Apalachicola Gold

Michael Kinnett

Published by:
Southern Yellow Pine (SYP) Publishing
4351 Natural Bridge Rd.
Tallahassee, FL 32305

All Rights reserved. No part of this publication may be reproduced, stored in a retrieval system, or transmitted in any form or by any means, electronic, mechanical, photocopying, recording, scanning or otherwise, without the prior written permission of the Publisher. For permission or further information contact SYP Publishing, LLC. 4351 Natural Bridge Rd., Tallahassee, FL 32305.

www.syppublishing.com

This is a work of fiction. Names, characters, places, and events that occur either are the products of the author's imagination or are used fictitiously. Any resemblance to actual persons, places, or events is purely coincidental.

The contents and opinions expressed in this book do not necessarily reflect the views and opinions of Southern Yellow Pine Publishing, nor does the mention of brands or trade names constitute endorsement.

ISBN-10: 1-940869-97-8
ISBN-13: 978-1-940869-97-1
ISBN-13: ePub 978-1-940869-98-8
Library of Congress Control Number: 2017935703

Copyright © 2017 by Michael A. Kinnett
Front Cover Design: Gina Smith
Photo credits listed individually pages 161-162

Printed in the United States of America
First Edition
March 2017

Dedication

To The Pearl of My Life,
My Granddaughter,
Olivia.

Also by Michael Kinnett

Apalachicola Pearl

Preface

At times, looked upon as a common, precocious, whelp, bastard child, and Lamb of God, LaRaela Retsyo Agnusdei, better known as Pearl, was a powerful force of change. As a young girl, Pearl possessed a spirit and grit that altered perceptions and changed the face of slavery in the Florida panhandle.

After stumbling upon a hidden treasure, Pearl possessed an enormous fortune. Pearl found no value in gold, for she sought greater treasure—a family.

Please enjoy as you follow Pearl's quest to find a father and mother in an attempt to create the family of her dreams. The War of Rebellion, a murderous father, and border ruffians are all that stand in her way.

The telling of this story begins in the present-day with the discovery of two journals I found hidden beneath a floorboard in the attic of the Orman House Museum. I completed the first journal and presented it to you with the title, *Apalachicola Pearl,* the writings of Michael Brandon Kohler. The second journal I present to you now. These are the writings of LaRaela Retsyo Agnusdei who was known to most as Pearl.

Michael Kinnett

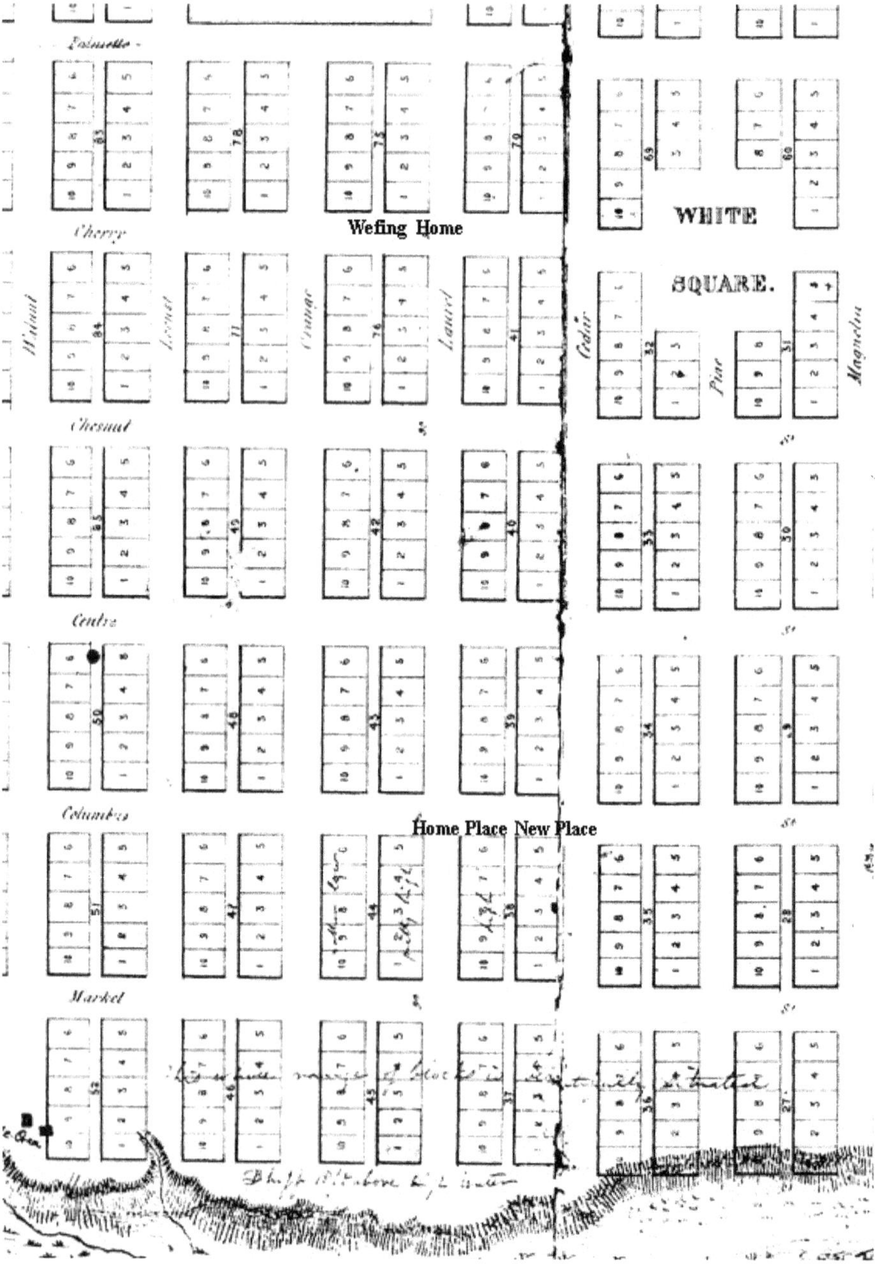
Cherry
Wefing Home
WHITE
SQUARE.
Walnut
Locust
Laurel
Cedar
Pine
Magnolia
Chesnut
Centre
Columbus
Home Place New Place
Market

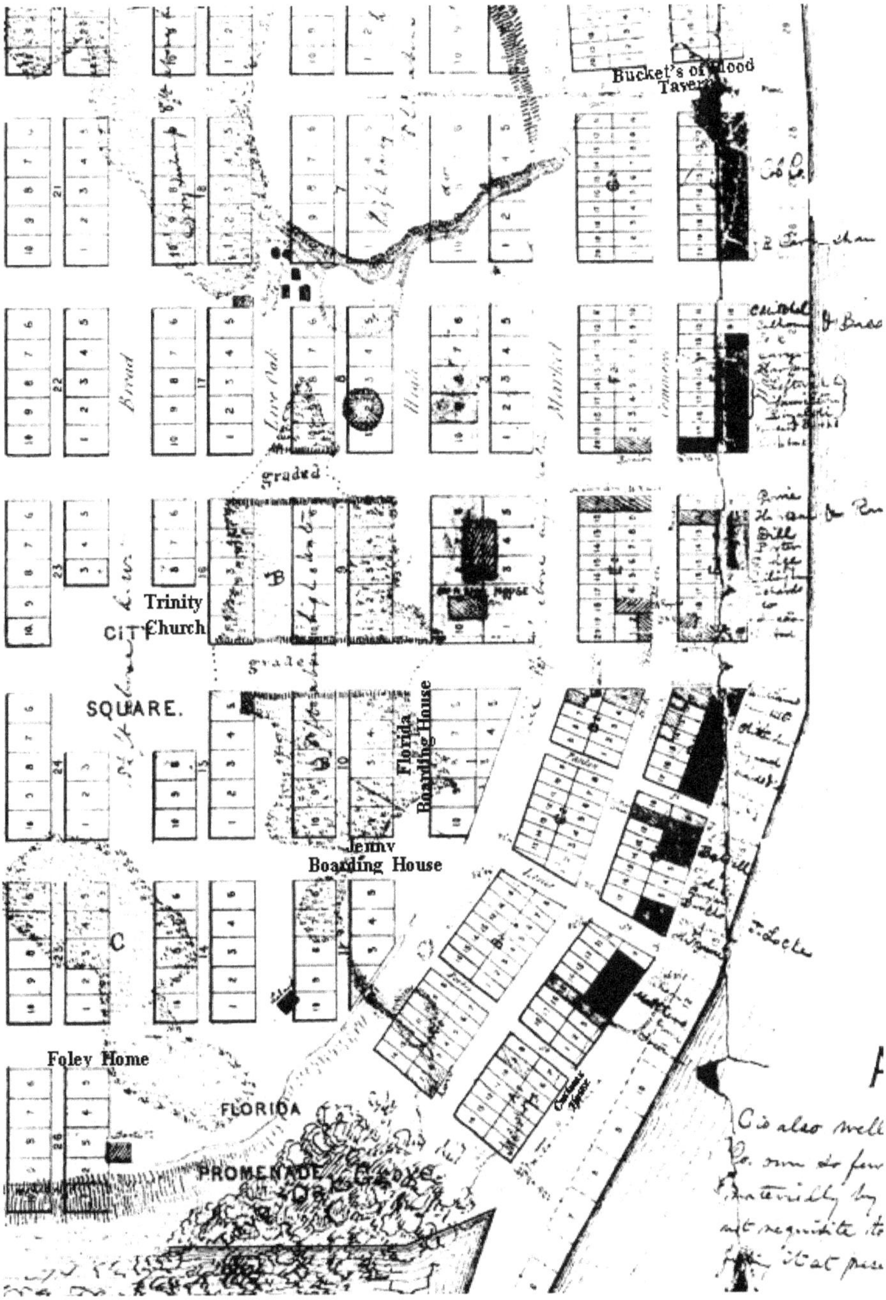
Bucket's of Blood Tavern
Trinity Church
CITY
SQUARE.
Florida Boarding House
Jenny Boarding House
Foley Home
FLORIDA
PROMENADE
graded
graded
Broad
Market

Chapter I

"There but for the Grace of God Go I"

"What is your earliest memory?" I asked the other children. They replied describing a picnic, a trip on a riverboat, and one recalled a ride on a mule. To me, these were recent memories, and I puzzled why they could not recall the beginning. I can remember first light and my mother's face the night of my birth, just before she died.

In a letter my mother left for me, I learned that I entered the world with my eyes wide open. Unaware of circumstance and with no words, my memories are held in image and emotion. From birth, a baby can distinguish the emotions of love and hate. My father taught me the opposite of love and hate by showing me his indifference.

I have a faded daguerreotype of my mother, and she was a beautiful woman. For many years, it troubled me that the image I held in my mind was of a different face. After witnessing the birth of a slave child, I could see the toll it took on the mother, and I understood. I remember being held tightly and her kindly eyes looking upon me. The voice of my mother flowed like a gentle melody to my ears, and I felt no fear.

The face of my father was to the contrary. His voice, course and loud, upset me, and I cried. My mother held me close; I suckled at my mother's breast and slumbered. I never saw my mother again.

Over the years, I have developed an unwavering faith in God, although after studying many religions, I am no longer sure of his name. I do know a benevolent creator exists simply because I was. Looking back, I would describe my young life as precariously balanced just above the edge of a razor. Each time I fell toward the edge, I was given a path, a narrow escape. It may have been that heaven, like my family, didn't want a common little whelp like me, so I was thrown back into the fray. I preferred to believe the creator designed a greater plan for my life. To survive, I clung to my hope and sought a higher destiny.

I lived in a sea of black faces, nurtured by and suckled at the breasts of plantation midwives. I thank God for the instincts of my black mothers, for in their eyes, I was not white but only a child. These midwives believed as was written in Mathew 18:3:

> "Unless you are converted and become as little children, you will by no means enter the kingdom of heaven."

Innocent and with a clean soul, I was cared for without judgment until an age of accountability when I'd chose my own path.

In the eyes of the law, I was a bastard. My father, Guillaume Gauthier Verheist, refused to give me his name and instead placed upon me the burden of my mother's death. I assumed the last name of my mother's family and was thus christened, LaRaela Retsyo Agnusdei. My mother called me Pearl.

The date of my birth is unclear. Judging by my size, I'd imagine 1854. Judging by how dull witted I found other children my size, 1852 was most likely when I, Pearl, opened my eyes into this world and so, "There but for the grace of God go I."

We traveled the coastline from New Orleans to Pensacola and north as far as Columbus, Georgia. My father owned a dray, the name given a flatbed cargo wagon and team of mules. By all outward appearances, he was a simple drayman hauling freight. He was known by most as "Dray," after his profession. The harsh truth is he was a murderous man who killed and stole at will.

Faith of a child is my plea when I seek forgiveness for my ignorance of his cruel ways. Unheeded and many times abandoned, I grew up alone or cared for by others. I did not know this man I called Father.

"Ordained destiny is seldom one we would choose. Living within our appointed destiny, knowing no other becomes our standard, and we accept it as our life." Pearl

I remember my father's words, scalding like a hot iron when drunken he cursed and cried out, "You may be white, but you always gonna be a no-good nigger for killin' your maw." His words seared into my mind, became a truth—a hard row to hoe for a child of four. I could not understand the hate in his words because I knew many Negros. They were my family, and I knew none that were "no good."

Where I grew up, death was always near. Preachers preached to help prepare for the inevitable, but grievers still wept at gravesides. To the poor, two ages were most important, the first being the age of one. Graveyards were filled with the markers of children unable to reach the end of the first year. Make it past one, and you may live to see forty. Any time past that was a gift from God.

Many times, I found myself scrutinizing over the remains of some unfortunate soul, lying in the woods or floating up on the bank of the river. Fevers claimed countless number of victims up and down the coastline. Many disappeared, swallowed by the land and water, never to be seen again.

Father taught me to check the pockets of the dead because in his words, "Those ignorant bastards don't need that shit no more." When my father collected enough coins, he left me for days at a time. He was not a generous man. It was best for me to hide a few coins back for food.

Early on, Father made a visit to my aunt near New Orleans where he tried to relieve himself of me, his burden. She refused to accept me into the family, fearing I would not fit in with her beautiful daughters. After a few days, Father relented, and we moved on to the east. It was during the visit with my aunt and cousins that my eyes were opened. My future became uncertain, and I had to learn to live with a sense of dread.

Like my aunt, the cousins commanded a beautiful facade, but beneath the shallow covering lay black hearts and clouded minds.

"Your mama's a Gypsy Witch. Did you know that Pearl?" Aida, scathingly questioned as she turned to her little sister for confirmation. "Ain't that right, Carina?"

Carina, with deceit in her eyes and a foreboding little smile on her face, kept silent, shaking her head in agreement. Taken by surprise, unable to confirm or deny, I held my tongue. For the time being, they had the upper hand. The cousins continued with the onslaught of verbal innuendos throughout the visit. I quickly grew tired of Aida's voice and Carina's smug little face.

Aunt Etta kept a clean but unsettling house. My Uncle Zenzo died of the fever shortly after the birth of Carina. At the time, I wondered if, instead of the fever, he simply looked upon his new daughter and died from the shock of what he created. The thought made me smile.

The house was filled with strangeness. Long dead creatures with eyes frozen in time stared down on those who entered. Sideboards filled with jars of strange concoctions and racks of dried plants gave the house a strong odor of herbs. Strange, old books, with hand written letters stuffed between their pages, filled the shelves. The books contained images of terrifying creatures and evil signs and symbols. I looked at some of the letters, but they were unreadable, written in the language of the old country.

I preferred to believe the embellishment of the house dated to my former Uncle Zenzo. It would have made more sense, knowing that men have darker tastes and seemed to prefer their animals dead and stuffed rather than alive. Unfortunately, it soon became apparent the house reflected the sensitivities of my Aunt Etta. I found this revelation disturbing to say the least.

My father and aunt spoke late into the nights, arguing over my fate. I laid quiet and still, listening and watching through a metal grate in the floor of my upstairs room. I had a good memory, and it served me well, holding on to the words and emotions so I might better sort them out in the light of day.

My aunt and father both tread lightly when it came to the concerns of my mother. It was as though she was in the room, and they struggled to converse using twisted remarks to state their cases, the words carefully crafted as though trying not to offend her. After the conversation ended, one certainty became apparent; my mother held a position of great power in this family.

Also apparent were Etta's feelings of envy and contempt. Neither my father nor my aunt supported the power she held in the family. In their trembling words, I found my saving grace. It made no difference if she was alive or a spirit among the dead—they both feared my mother. According to the laws of my family, when certain events occurred in the stars, I would assume her power.

I did not comprehend the unseen powers that protected me. Their talk of the dead and spirits watching over me was quite unnerving. I preferred to think my protection came from the living, perhaps my mother's brothers, my four uncles, but what was the difference between the living and the dead? I knew less of my uncles than I did of the spirits.

The conversation continued over the next three nights, and my cousins continued to pester me in the waking hours. I listened carefully, piecing together a plan to survive. The talk on the fourth night sent chills down my spine.

"You know Guillaume, heaven forbid if the fates were to frown on Pearl, and I would have to carry my sister's burden in the family. I, of course, would seek you out for comfort," Etta luridly stated.

"What about the curse?"

"To hell with the curse. Are you a man or a coward?" Etta screamed under her breath.

"Easy for you! I carry the burden of the child along with the curse every day." Father scowled back.

In a calmer voice, Etta said, "You just need to take time and weigh your options. I'm sure you will make the right choice, one beneficial to both of us."

"I just don't know." Shaking his head, Father replied, "How can I get out from under this curse?"

"You need to keep an eye on our Pearl. A young girl left unattended in some of the places you frequent could come to harm. Of course, it wouldn't be any fault of yours if the fates played a role and something tragic were to happen," Etta, shrewdly suggested.

I rolled onto my back and pulled a blanket up to my chin. I laid shivering as their words ran through my mind.

Early the next morning, my father called out and told me to come along. The wagon was packed and the team already hitched. We stood in the parlor and said our goodbyes, my father hugging and whispering to Etta, looked over her shoulder to me. I was in the hall stroking the feathers of a stuffed raven that sat on the hall table. Etta believed ravens held the spirits of the dead, allowing them to keep vigilance over the living. I didn't believe such nonsense. I spoke quietly to the bird. My conversation was simple and one of sadness over his fate. No one else could have heard my words.

We left the house, but as we approached the wagon, a raven flew down from a tree and landed on the seatback above where I sat. Father froze in his tracks and glared at the raven. The raven, silent, glared back. I watched as my father turned pale. The fates were with me this day, and an old crow had just bought me some time.

As for my two annoying cousins, I left a parting gift. In the pages of those old books were many odd symbols and disturbing images. Not comprehending the meaning, I took the strangest of the symbols and using burned charcoal from the fireplace, I made a rendering on the floor of their bedroom. In the center of the symbol, I stuck a candle.

Months later, Father severely scolded me for the deed, but from that day on, except twice, he never raised a hand to me. Aunt Etta and my two beautiful cousins never spent another night in that house. I could not fathom what it was I had done, but it made me smile.

Chapter II

In the Eye of the Beast

Travel was hard, but I loved every second of the journey. Keep quiet and be respectful, and my father would leave me alone.

The wagon swayed as we moved along trails created long before Europeans by the ancestors of the Creek and Apalachee tribes. Old Spanish mission trails were among the best roads, but at times, we traveled on no more than a cattle trail or animal track, making our way across the panhandle.

We boarded steamers and barges to cross rivers. At times, even with water up to the wagon bed, the mules plodded along roads flooded by swollen streams. They found their way by instinct as though the water was not even there.

The forests, swamps, and wetlands were filled with creatures of every description, most of which, at one time or the other, I have eaten. I say this with a heavy heart, having held some creatures of beauty and grace in high regard.

Towns and cities lay waiting at journey's end. Living creatures unto themselves, made up of hundreds and sometimes thousands of people choosing to live side by side. Individuals going about separate tasks but supporting the whole as though controlled by a single mind.

These were my most special places in the world. I could start talking to people first thing in the morning and go nonstop till dark. My favorite city was Apalachicola, Florida. It wasn't the largest, but in my mind, these were the finest people in my world.

During the time of Spanish rule, the delta lands were known as Murder Point. It was early settlers that renamed the transient settlement Cottonton. As it became a more permanent settlement, the name West Point seemed more appropriate and indicated that it sat on the west side of the bay. Soon, the town of West Point would change once again to share the name of the river it served. Apalachicola during the 1830s and 1840s was a Gulf Coast, cotton-shipping, boom town surpassed only by Mobile, Alabama and New Orleans, Louisiana.

There were three rivers that fed the waters of the Apalachicola. The Chattahoochee was the largest. The waters of the Chattahoochee began their journey in the Blue Ridge Mountains of Northeast Georgia. From there, they cut their way across the land to Atlanta, soon after forming the border separating Georgia from Alabama, a benefit to both states.

The Flint River began its journey just below Atlanta, traveling through the cotton country of West Central Georgia and eventually crossing into Florida where it joined with the Chattahoochee to form the Apalachicola River.

The Chipola was the smallest, but to those living in lower Southeastern Alabama and Northwest Florida, it was an artery to the Gulf of Mexico, feeding the economy. The Chipola was ninety-three miles long and joined with the Apalachicola just above the city through a web of waterways and swamps.

The Apalachicola of the 1850s, although still the third largest shipping port on the Gulf Coast, was in decline. Twice the cotton was being grown to the north, but cotton receipts remained at a stagnate level. Apalachicola citizens began searching for the next new opportunity, and they did so with a spirit and drive that I found inspiring.

Trying to escape the hurricane of fifty-two, the side-wheeler *Albany,* ran aground on Scipio Creek just north of Apalachicola. Her hull was ripped apart by the knees of the great cypress trees. She was beyond salvage. With her boiler and hardware long since removed, the derelict steamer, once a center of activity, lay quietly along the bank of the wetlands. When father worked the cotton season in Apalachicola, the *Albany* was the special place I called home.

Albany

Her bow sat nestled in the tree line, impaled on cypress knees, her stern forever trapped in the muck and reeds. Excepting storm tides, the hull rarely drew more water than to my elbow, but just past the stern, the water deepened into a channel that sounded one to six fathoms. It was through these many channels we navigated the delta wetlands to and from the city of Apalachicola.

I graded her fair to middling as far as plumb although I once dropped some peas on her bow, and they quickly picked up speed to the stern. In the eye of a child who expected nothing, the *Albany's* accommodation was equal to the finest hotel I could have imagined.

We feasted well on an abundance of fish, oysters, and crabs from the channel and bay. The woodland held a bounty of nuts, berries, quince, and loquat. I soon proclaimed myself queen of these watery lands.

My father scolded me to stay put while he worked, but a day is an eternity to a child, so I wandered. I often walked the trails through the woodland the two miles to town, but the thought of becoming dinner to a panther made me a little squeamish, and I preferred rowing a mile by water.

A skiff was our main boat for transport. Father used the skiff getting to the mainland where he kept the dray and mules. Unknown to my father, I made do with a small dinghy I had salvaged from the *Albany* and kept hidden in the reeds near shore.

I was five or six when I began wandering the streets of Apalachicola. There was a large board that stood near the court house where people posted notices and bills. I sat on a bench near the board, watching as one person read a notice and others listened. I knew that if a word was long when spoken, it took more letters to write. When people drifted away, I looked at the same notice and repeated what they had just said, following the words on the paper with my finger. This is how I taught myself to read and write.

I remember the first time I stood with my mouth gaping open, looking up at the pillars of the Trinity Episcopal Church. I was drawn by unknown forces to enter the sanctuary. With eyes as big as saucers, I tried to comprehend the majesty of this palace. I fully expected God himself to enter from the back and ask me what I was doing there.

Trinity Episcopal Church, Apalachicola, Florida

Suddenly, there was a sound so loud and so deep my teeth vibrated in my head. My eyes shifted to colossal pipes running clear to the top of the great hall. That was when I noticed an old man smiling and peeking around a large wooden box. I just knew it had to be him—God.

My voice was silenced, and my bare feet held fast to the floor as God stood and approached down the center aisle. Overwrought, I stood in the presence of God and fainted.

When my eyes once again opened, I just knew I had been transported to heaven. I lay on a bench with my head resting on God's lap, looking up through the branches of a live oak tree. God had one hand on the back of the bench and in the other was holding and reading from a copy of the book he had written called, "The Bible."

God looked down on me kindly. "Are you alright child?" he asked.

"Yes, God," I responded.

Noticeably amused, he smiled. "I'm not God, child, but I do work for him. You can call me Vicar."

Sitting up, I asked, "Is Vicar your whole name?"

"Well not really; my given name is Horace Rutledge, but people just call me Vicar because that's who I am when I work for God," said the Vicar.

"Pleased to meet you, Vicar." I boldly extended my hand to shake. Once again, the Vicar was noticeably amused. I told him, "I understand about your name; you and I have the same kinda' problem. My name is really LaRaela Retsyo Agnusdei, but everybody calls me Pearl…, but I don't work for God."

I didn't understand why, but the Vicar began laughing out loud, and his eyes started watering as though he was crying. Eventually, he calmed himself, and the first thing he did was give me a big hug and thank me for nothing.

This would be the first of many visits to my new friend the Vicar. He was a good man who helped me with my reading and writing, and he was always full of good advice.

During our visits, I tried to explain to the Vicar Rutledge that hunger is a good teacher when it comes to rolling drunks and picking pockets. I told him the pain of hunger was stronger than the inner voice of the conscience he kept talking about. He spent the afternoon trying to convince me otherwise. I eventually relented just to let him off the hook.

Soon after my first visit with the Vicar, no matter where I was sitting in town, people began walking up, introducing themselves, and striking up a conversation. I started carrying an old croker sack because people were always giving me food, little candies, and cakes, many times sharing their noon meal with me. It was wonderful having so many interesting people to talk with. It was nice not being alone.

It was a bitter day for me when I first realized many fathers cherished their daughters. This revelation came shortly after another of my father's drunken tirades. I was having trouble making sense of my father's antagonism and anger toward me. The Vicar assured me I was not at fault and that it was just what they called a coincidence that my mother died the same day I was born. It was also the same day he revealed to me I was neither mulatto nor a slave.

It was my experience that Jesus viewed a slave much as the old widow in the story when she dropped two copper coins in the collection box. Jesus praised her to his disciples because although poor, she gave all she had. My black family seemed to be closer to God in a shack with a dirt floor than many whites were in a grand manor house. Unable to read many quoted, long scriptures from memory, they carried the words in their hearts. I shared my thoughts with the Vicar, and in time, he cried with me over the plight of my black family.

I was glad the cotton season started in December. I was never happier than the evenings I spent sitting in the sanctuary at Trinity with baby Jesus, among all of the holiday trappings.

Too soon, Christmas ended, and in a city built by cotton and commerce, it became all hands on deck. These were exciting times.

December, January, and February were winter in the panhandle; most years were crisp but bearable. The cooler weather was a small price to pay to be rid of the fevers and the bothersome insects. The tavern, Buckets of Blood, known to most as just Blood's Tavern, generally kept a fire burning on the street on cooler evenings. I would sit on a bucket near the fire, waiting for my father to drink his medicine. It was here I was given the nickname Prickly Pear for the jackknives I carried to keep the drunks at bay.

Even here in this pit of despair, I had a friend. The rather large man pouring drinks was a man they called Basher. Basher was as big as a cotton bale with a heart to match his size. He had a daughter he doted on and treasured above all else. Bella and I were about the same age.

Some nights, father took too much of the medicine and fell asleep or if it was very cold, Basher collected me from the street. His daughter Bella and I played in the back room of the tavern.

Some nights, Bella's mom didn't have to work, and she stayed home with Bella. Basher still collected me from the street, allowing me to hide away in the cabinet under the bar. It was warm and safer than the street. There I could peek out from cracks of the bar and listen to those gathered, occasionally earning my keep by handing Basher glasses.

He told me never to touch the knife. It was hard not to because the handle was striking—made from the tooth of a sperm whale and scrimshawed with amazing images from when he worked as a whaler. The blade was formed from a broken saber. He kept the knife and a hickory club under the bar and grabbed one or the other, depending on the severity of the fights that inevitably broke out. Tonight, he needed both.

When the cards didn't fall in his favor, father began to rampage, overturning the table and drawing his knife. He was drunk out of his mind, ready to kill over the outcome of the card game. Basher responded in kind with the knife in his right hand and the club in his left. Father threatened Basher to stay out of it, but it was his job to keep the peace, and he was not one to back down.

Basher bested my father, taking his knife, knocking him unconscious, and dragging him into the street. It was here that Basher spoke with Constable Jacob Foley about the incident. Basher and Jacob were best of friends. Basher told me more than once that Mr. Foley was a man I could trust if I ever needed help.

When he returned to the bar, he knelt down, begged my forgiveness, and told me I must return home quickly and hide myself away till morning when my father would come to his senses.

This was why late on a moonlit night at the end of May, I found myself rowing frantically back to the *Albany*. I was trying to arrive by water before father arrived by land. It was my good fortune that, in his inebriated state, he was slow to find his way. I hid the dinghy in the reeds near shore.

Balancing on a plank, I boarded the bow of the *Albany*. As I walked back to climb the stairs to my cabin, I heard a drone deeper than the lowest note of the Trinity pipes. It was a mournful, pulsating sound, evoking feelings of both fear and misfortune.

The *Albany's* lower deck just past the boiler mounts opened to the stern for cargo and passengers. Shaded from the moonlight by the upper deck, it lay before me in shadow.

The *Albany* carried a width of twenty-eight feet and a length of near one fifty, making my journey back long, dark, and frightening.

Just short of the stern the main beams were broken, and the deck planking bowed, angling down into the channel. With every step, the moon became more visible below the upper deck, illuminating my path.

It was here on the stern I spotted a dark object laying on the deck. Its form was obscured by a light mist rising from the water. As I grew closer, it appeared as though a log drifting down the channel had lodged on the planking. Perhaps the sound was from the rough bark scraping on the deck as the log moved in the current.

Standing near, I reached out and touched the side of the log, feeling no bark but rather a tangle of netting and heavy cord. Relieved, I took a deep breath and decided to deal with this in the morning, but as I turned, the moaning began again, and to my terror, the enormous tail of a gator curled onto the deck.

I stood unable to move, awaited the worst, but nothing happened. When I finally came to myself, I slowly backed up to starboard and lit a camphene lantern. Holding the lantern high, I approached the great beast. He was over a rod in length with the girth of a cypress tree. It occurred to me that I could be in the presence of the legendary gator called Old Hickory.

The great beast lay at my feet. In the light of my lantern, I began feeling more pity than fear. Tangled in snare lines and heavy netting, he could scarcely move.

It was in his nature to roll in the water, trying to free himself, but instead of freedom, his instinct served to form an unyielding rope of tightly wound netting that followed him like an anchor, holding him back and dragging him under. With four arrows protruding from his back and tail, this creature was exhausted to the point of death. I can nary imagine a battle so fierce to have brought Old Hickory to my doorstep.

The voice inside me may have screamed flee, but my heart went out to the great beast. I knew of bondage and had no tolerance of it, having seen many of my black family held by rope and chain and restrained by devises I cannot begin to describe. Being a child, I watched and suffered in silence, held back by others who also had no choice, but this night, I had a choice.

I was of good heart, but most people would have considered me lacking in good sense when I began the task of saving this beast. His back was coarse. I likened it to an enormous wood rasp used by a giant in a story book.

I threw a section of heavy canvas over his back that I might climb aboard and move around. He lay so still I felt he might have already perished, but soon, I felt his heart pounding through the shafts as I twisted, pulling the arrows from his flesh. I cannot imagine the number of days he must have spent struggling under the weight of the nets, trying to free himself. Spent, laboring to draw a breath, Hickory seemed resolved that his life would be forfeited here on the stern of the *Albany*.

An eerie feeling fell upon me as it became apparent I was being watched. Along the shore, out in the channel and near the tall reeds, the lantern light revealed a multitude of glowing red eyes probing the darkness. They gathered, sensing a feast was near.

The misfortune of one would be celebrated by many if Hickory were to perish on this night.

Pulling a jackknife from my pocket, I cut at the snare lines, and they soon slid from his back, dragged into the channel by the weight of the net. Unafraid, I sat looking into his eyes, speaking gently, stroking his snout.

The stench of alcohol alerted me to Father's presence as he nervously watched from the darkness. Hickory soon regained his senses and slid back into the water.

Like the raven, to Father, it was a sign of my growing power. It never occurred to him it should be a sign of acceptance. The snares binding Father's heart were ones I could not cut.

To him, the outcome of my encounter must have been disappointing and served as a warning that he needed to proceed with his and Etta's plan with even greater caution.

Chapter III

Charity

    Father packed and left the next morning without a word, leaving me to my own means. Not knowing when or if he would return, now, I spent my days in Apalachicola.

    Early each morning, I rowed the dinghy down Scipio Creek to just north of town. Hiding my boat in the needle rush, I followed a path though the wetlands, beat the vegetation with my snake stick, and warned them to stay away. The path led to the start of High Street just behind the home known as the Orman House.

    A slave shack sat behind the main house near the street where I passed by. It was here I heard a voice.

    "Oh my, oh my, Miss Charity. How you ever gonna' get caught up?" the voice exclaimed. "I just don't know what you gonna' do to be finished on time," the same voice replied.

    I stood listening to the conversation, but there seemed to be only one person. The exchange made me smile. Soon an old black woman appeared on the porch with a canvas bag in tow, and she looked right at me.

    "Hello there child," she kindly said.

    "Hello," I replied back.

    "Who ya talkin' to?" I asked.

    "Why I is just talkin' to the only smart person round till you come along." And she and I both stood chuckling until our eyes watered.

Miss Charity's shack. Drawn by Olivia years later.

"Why, I think I know you girl. You must be Miss Pearl," Miss Charity stated.

"How you know my name?" I asked, looking at her as though she could read minds.

"Why, we both know some of the same people. The Vicar an old friend to Miss Charity, and he done told me all about you. He think you purdy special," Charity replied.

"How come you so far behind in your work that you need be frettin' and carryin' on?" I asked.

"I got to do all the laundry for Mr. Orman today, and I got no help," Charity replied, shaking her head in despair.

"You don't got to be worried. I'll help you," and with that I walked over and grabbed hold of that canvas bag of dirty clothes. I couldn't figure out why she needed help; there wasn't that much laundry. The clothes were finished and drying on the line before noon, and she did most of the work herself.

With the work now well in hand, we sat on the porch of her shack, passing the time of day. I sat gawking in amazement when she pulled a fancy pipe from her apron, struck a match, and began puffing. I'd never seen a woman smoking a pipe before.

I gasped when from around the side of the big house a lady appeared, and she was wearing the most beautiful dress I'd ever seen. She walked right up and began talking to Miss Charity. She was truly the most enchanting lady I'd ever come across—not that in my short life I'd come across too many.

"Miss Sadie, I declare you are a vision to behold," Charity said.

"Thank you, Miss Charity. I hope you and your guest are enjoying this most pleasant of days," she replied.

"Why thank you kindly for asking. Miss Pearl and I are havin' a wonderful visit."

Turning her attention to me, Miss Sadie declared, "It is so nice to make your acquaintance Miss Pearl. If you would forgive me for being so bold, may I inquire why a beautiful young lady such as yourself would be wearing boy's clothes?

"I don't got no dresses," I replied, blushing. No one ever called me beautiful before.

"I do not currently have any dresses would be the more appropriate response, but not to worry, we can work on that later," Miss Sadie responded. Handing me a box from under her arm, Miss Sadie motioned that I should look inside. The box contained two dresses, both about my size.

"These are dresses I have outgrown. They are in very good condition; would you be allowed to take these and put them to good use, Miss Pearl?"

I was so busy stroking and admiring the dresses, I might not have been paying attention.

"Miss Charity, I believe I will leave the details of Miss Pearl's bath in your capable hands."

"Bath," I exclaimed. "You don't need to worry about that. I jumped in the river yesterday and got plenty wet," I explained.

Miss Charity and Miss Sadie both began to chuckle. "Why, Miss Pearl, didn't the Vicar ever tell you that cleanliness is next to Godliness?" Miss Sadie inquired.

"Yeah but…" was all I got out before Miss Charity took me by the hand and walked me to the building nearest the well. They couldn't have known I was coming. How wealthy they must have been to keep a tub of hot water ready for guests. How fortunate was I that Miss Sadie was walking around with those dresses under her arm? It was almost as though they knew I was coming.

Having already experienced a couple of baths in the past, I thought I knew what a bath was until I had one of Miss Charity's baths. She scrubbed me from stem to stern to within an inch of my life. You couldn't have found any dirt on me even if you tried. She even got the dirt from under my fingernails and toenails. She washed my hair and scrubbed my teeth. I never saw much advantage to using soap, but I had to admit, dirt came off easier, and I smelled wonderful.

I could have lived happily the rest of my life not having my hair combed out and put in that bun. When it was all over, Miss Charity dressed me, and we headed to the big house to show Miss Sadie.

The Orman's house was a palace without equal. I was sure those doorknobs were made of the finest of diamonds and gold. Miss Sadie was sitting on a sofa in the parlor when I walked in. Looking past me to Miss Charity, Miss Sadie exclaimed, "Why Miss Charity, where is Miss Pearl? Has she been called away? I am disappointed. I so wanted to see her in all of her finery. Who is this proper young lady I see before me?"

I think she must have known it was me, but she made such a fuss, I couldn't help but to smile and giggle. "It's me Miss Sadie…Pearl; don't you recognize me?"

Miss Sadie proceeded to put on a show, going on and on about me. Miss Charity soon chimed in with more of the same. I thought it was all for nothing until I was led to a tall mirror in the backroom, and I saw myself for the first time. I have to say it made all the tortures of preparations seem worthwhile. It seemed to make my common appearance more acceptable.

Miss Anna, Miss Sadie's mama, arrived home, and I was introduced as Miss Pearl. Having never met Miss Anna, I was surprised when the first words out of her mouth were, "What a lovely young lady." I was starting to think maybe they weren't just pulling my leg. I felt reborn. Before today, I could never have imagined being a young lady.

Miss Charity remained standing while I sat on the sofa and visited with Miss Sadie and Miss Anna. During our conversation, Miss Anna accused Miss Sadie of encouraging gossip and told her to quit being so incorrigible. Miss Anna became frustrated when Miss Sadie continued to ask me about the goings on in town, prying deeper into the affairs of others. Miss Anna left shaking her head, preferring to sew in the next room, and it was from here she occasionally chuckled and made comments.

From that time on, I preferred girl clothes; it became a rare sight to see me in trousers. More dresses would follow, and Miss Sadie eventually set a wardrobe up in Miss Charity's shack for me to keep my things.

I dressed each morning at Miss Charity's. She helped me with my buttons and hair, making me presentable for the day. I was required to take a bath at least once a week, and I had to learn to take care of my own clothes. It was Miss Charity who taught me to take care of myself. Miss Charity became my mother.

There were days when Miss Charity suffered from the decrepitude. I felt privileged when she relied on me to help her through the bad days.

***

The Vicar was very impressed with my new appearance. I once told him I wished I was prettier. He told me God only cared that I was clean and polite. I guess two of the three wasn't all that bad. He was so proud of me, he walked me straight down to the restaurant at the Florida Boarding House to celebrate with a meal and a piece of pie.

Here, he introduced me to Miss Caroline, the owner. I was told Miss Caroline had recently misplaced her husband and was looking for help. I first offered to help her look for the husband she claimed to have lost, but that offer was met with a tear and a smile. She told me helping her around the restaurant would be good enough. She paid me for helping with two meals a day and pie. The Vicar said he thought it was a good deal.

Bella didn't recognize me until I spoke, and Basher was staggering around as though he were about to pass out at the sight of me in a dress. Basher was very happy to see me; since his encounter with father, he had been fretting that I'd no longer view him as my friend. Basher was wrong about that. It was he who didn't understand about my father. I told him it did my heart good to see Father get his comeuppance. Having experienced my father's wrath many times before, I warned Basher to take caution.

***

Evening found me sitting atop the pilot's house of the *Albany*, watching the sunsets. God's palette never ceased to amaze me. Birds of all descriptions soared above, and all manner of creatures made occasional appearances as they passed by land or water. It was peaceful until the mosquitoes began rising for a nightly feast. It was time to hide away in my cabin, covering my bed with the gauze and lace I had collected.

I considered myself fortunate to have so many friends and lucky to be eating so well. Father had been gone a week, and it began to trouble me to spend my nights alone, not out of fear, but of loneliness. With such new and caring friends, this was the first time in my life I'd felt truly alone.

Not knowing when Father would return, I thought it best to accept Miss Charity and Miss Caroline's invitations to spend my nights with them. Looking back, I relished the three nights I stayed at the Florida Boarding House. Miss Caroline had two helpers, Lottie and Ava, and between the four of us, the nights were filled with games, gossip, and laughter.

How could I go back to the way it was before? It was because of my new-found arrogance I committed one of my greatest sins—praying to God, my father would not return.

It had been the best two weeks of my life. With a new hope, I lay plans for a future that before, I could never have imagined.

Chapter IV

Bella was Dead

Bella was dead. I had seen death before but none that touched me so deeply.

Up early, I slipped out from Miss Charity's before she woke. Excited, I ran to the alley behind Blood's to meet up with Bella. We'd been making plans all week to spend the entire day together.

I thought Bella must have left the backdoor ajar, knowing I was coming. I knocked and called in, "Bella, it's just me Pearl; we'd better get going. Miss Caroline said she'd make us a breakfast." There was no reply, only a deafening silence.

I passed through the storage room and cracked open the door that led to the tavern. I peeked in behind the bar, and in a hushed voice, I called out, "Bella…Bella, are you in here?" The morning light was just breaking through the front windows as I made my way around the end of the counter.

Bella lay still on a table. The dress she wore the night before was ripped from her body, castoff, and hanging snagged on the back of a chair. Walking over, I laid my hand on her forehead. I wanted so badly to stroke her hair.

Bella had beautiful, long, black hair, but now matted, it flowed with her blood over the edge of the table. Bella's face, filled with terror, was held fast, locked in a moment of time. The blood came from a deep slit in her throat and covered the table and floor in a red pool.

I gazed into her eyes, but they were cold and dead. I could tell she was no longer in this body. Suddenly, in an instant, I was no longer in the bar; I was in the street, and someone was screaming.

My next memory was of standing in the street—I could hear screaming. Looking down at myself, I could not rationalize all of the blood. I was so careful, but my dress was covered in blood. I thought to myself, *Miss Charity will never be able to wash this blood out.* I brushed it with my hands, trying to get it off my dress, but now it was on my hands. I frantically rubbed my hands together, trying to get the blood off, but it wouldn't go away. That's when I realized, it was me who was screaming.

People began to rush over. I am unclear how long I screamed. My next memory was of looking into Miss Caroline's green eyes. She held my face in her hands, calling out, "Pearl, Pearl, look at me Pearl. Stay with me Pearl." Miss Caroline held me tightly and took me from that place.

It was as though my mind was shattered, and I was seeing in bits and pieces…Lottie pumping a well, Miss Caroline's hands scrubbing mine, Ava running with a blanket. In one moment awake, asleep in the next. Nothing was connected when suddenly, everything went black.

***

When I came to, it was mid-afternoon. I'd helped Lottie clean this room before, so I knew I was at the Florida Boarding House. Miss Caroline sat holding my hand and stroking my forehead. The Vicar stood to my right, looking very concerned, asking the same question he asked the first time we met. "Are you alright child?"

"Yes, Vicar. I'm alright," I answered, but my thoughts soon turned to Bella, and I started crying. Miss Caroline who didn't know Bella all that well began crying with me. She picked me up and held me close. At the time, I thought it nice of Miss Caroline to help me cry for Bella. It was later I realized she was crying for me.

That evening, a few people gathered on the porch to try and discover what happened. Miss Caroline insisted that it was too soon to ask me any questions. Sitting on the floor below the window, I could just make out what was being said. With an ear to the open window, I quietly listened.

Basher, now missing, stood accused by many of Bella's murder. It wasn't hard to hear when Constable Jacob Foley came to the defense of his friend, accusing some who had gathered of jumping to conclusions. "Just because Basher wasn't a church goer didn't make him a bad person," Jacob hollered.

I couldn't stand to hear talk like that, so I walked onto the porch and told those people, "You leave Basher alone. He loved Bella more than you love God. He would never hurt her. He would die himself before he would let anything bad happen to any child. Basher is my friend. Leave him alone, and look for who really did this."

I tried so hard to hold in my tears, but the image of Bella haunted me, and I fell to my knees crying. Again, Miss Caroline picked me up and held me close. She turned and scolded those gathered, sending them away. I watched as they left. Constable Foley looked back at me, and I could tell by his eyes, he would not rest until Basher was found and cleared of those malicious allegations.

I insisted on going to the graveside service to hear the Vicar. Bella's mom was inconsolable. I hugged her, hoping it would give her some comfort, but like me, she couldn't stop being sad. The Vicar did a good job, and I was sure his words paved a path so Bella could find her way to Jesus.

Jacob Foley kept his word, and shortly after Bella's funeral, Basher was cleared of all suspicion. Basher's body was discovered lodged on an oyster bar behind St. George Island. Basher's hands were tied behind his back. He had been bludgeoned to death, and like Bella, his throat was slit just for good measure.

Although sickened by the news, my tears were spent. I quietly slipped away from the crowd, wandering back toward the *Albany*. I needed time to myself to try and sort things out. I should have told someone I was leaving, but I didn't want them talking me out of it.

Hiding the dinghy in the grass, I climbed the narrow plank onto the bow of the *Albany*. From my cabin, I gathered my few possessions into a bag and from the upper deck dropped the bag onto the bow. Turning, I climbed to the top of the pilot house to say goodbye to my watery kingdom. My mind was made up. I was returning to Apalach to try and make a better life for myself. With all the happenings going on, I no longer felt safe.

Halfway down the plank, I was startled, almost losing my balance.

"Where the hell you think you're goin' girl?" my father asked.

"Papa, you're back," I exclaimed with not the slightest hint of a smile on my face.

"Yeah, and I'll just bet you're happy to see me too. What the hell you wearin' girl? You steal that fancy dress?" Father scowled.

"No father; it was given to me," I responded.

"Poor attempt at turnin' a sow's ear into a silk purse to my concerns. Get back on that boat girl. You ain't goin' nowhere tonight," and he followed me back up the plank.

"I was plannin' to move into town, so I wouldn't be troublin' you no more," I told him.

"Don't be frettin' about that; I have done took care of that," was the last thing he said. I returned to my cabin, doubling over because of the knot in my stomach. Returning to the *Albany* forever haunted me.

My father never lifted a finger to help me do anything. I know he considered me his bastard child. I once believed that, at the very least, it was because of him I was not an orphan. I considered it sad that this was his only redeeming quality, but now I could see there was a life beyond my father.

At first light, father yelled to get a move on, and we headed to town through the wood. I asked him, "Why ain't we takin' the skiff?"

"You askin' too many questions Pearl. You need to learn to keep your mouth shut. Bad things can happen to a child and her friends if'n she talks too much." Father gave me a look that sent chills down the center of my back. I walked quietly the rest of the way back to town.

Father left on a steamer heading up river but told me he'd be back by seven and to meet him outside of Blood's. I figured he didn't know about Bella and Basher yet, and I didn't say anything to encourage a conversation. At this point, I just wanted him to go away.

Miss Caroline was overjoyed when I came walkin' up the steps at the boarding house. You'd of thought I was a long-lost relative. She scolded me for worrying her and said she had half the town out looking for me. I was very sad to tell her my father returned, and I wouldn't be staying with her for a while. She started crying and hugged me.

I stayed with Miss Caroline till ten o'clock, leaving to let Miss Charity know I was okay. Miss Charity made the same big fuss, and if that wasn't enough, Miss Sadie and Miss Anna came out of the big house, and I had to hear it all again. I didn't mind though. I could tell by their concern they loved and cared for me.

I had lots to do before the end of June when the cotton season would close, and father and I would be traveling, picking up odd jobs during the fall and winter.

Chapter V

Pirates

    Miss Charity had to get on with her duties for the Orman family, so I wandered away down to an old building that sat on the corner of the Orman property. I was looking for a place to do some thinking and lay out a plan.
    The scary, old building was given the name Charity House back in the early days when it served as a nunnery and was nothing to do with Miss Charity. I explored the building inside and out. There were two rooms, and they were full of Mr. Orman's junk, stuff that was not good enough to use but was too good to throw away.
    There was a lot of undergrowth to contend with as I made my way around the foundation. One, old water oak was growing so close to the building, the trunk pushed the bricks up and busted the foundation. I circled the tree, but as I got to the other side, the ground gave way and my left foot fell in a hole up to my knee. It was strange though; the hole kept collapsing deeper and deeper, and as I listened, the debris seemed to be falling into a hollow chamber beneath the building.
    "Curiosity killed the cat," the Vicar once told me.
    "But satisfaction brought it back," I finished his quote. I had to know what was down there, in the darkness, beneath the Charity House.

    Everyone, except a couple of slaves working the gardens had left for the day, and I knew they wouldn't say anything because they were used to seeing me around. I slipped into Orman's mule barn, grabbed a camphene lantern and twine, and returned to the Charity House, occasionally looking back to make sure no one saw me.

I tied the twine to the lantern's bail, lit the wick, and lowered the lantern into the hole. I needed to see where I was going. This close to wetlands, I had no intentions of running into a moccasin in the dark. The lantern dropped about a fathom and came to rest at the bottom of the hole. With no snakes in sight, all I needed to do was work up enough nerve to follow the lantern.

Taking a deep breath, I climbed down using the roots of the tree as a ladder. It was a tight fit, but I managed to squeeze between the tree roots and the foundation. I was glad I wore my trousers. This was no job for a dress.

The foundation extended into the ground less than an arm's length; from there a thick layer of soil continued down to a heavy stone wall. Over the years, a large root from the water oak tree, pushing against the wall, compromised its integrity, and a few of the stones fell into a chamber. Holding the lantern close to my face, I peered through a hole in the stone wall.

The wall was constructed of two layers of ballast stones held in place with tabby mortar made of sand and ground oyster shells. I used my foot to kick the remaining loose stones into the chamber, making it safer and giving me a larger hole to pass through.

Leaning into the opening, I lowered the lantern down into the chamber. It came to rest on a ledge not far from the opening. I entered the chamber backwards feet first. I was just long enough from the waist down that I could touch the ledge with my toes.

Upon closer inspection, I was surprised to find the ledge was a shelf made of heavy cypress planks. What looked like dirt and sand was a layer of sail cloth used to cover the contents of the shelf. Peering over, I again lowered my light to the floor of the chamber. A second shelf acted as a step, and I easily made my way down.

The floor was made of the same ballast stone as the walls, and the chamber was as dry as a tomb. I'd seen large chambers like this before in the old Spanish forts where they kept the powder. The ceiling was arched for strength to support the soil above, and together, they protected the black powder from cannon fire. The Charity House must have come much later, unknowingly built over the chamber.

The origins of the Charity House had been lost in the passing of time, perhaps built by the Spanish missionaries to minister to the local heathen tribes. No one could have imagined that hidden beneath its foundation lay this older relic.

The chamber was of good size, just shy of a rod in width and length. Two shelves of heavy cypress planks filled the walls. Each shelf was draped in heavy sail canvas.

The canvas was stiff; its edges crumbled in my hands as I pulled it from a lower shelf. I retrieved the lantern so I might see what was contained on the shelf. To my disappointment, it was filled with a stack of heavy metal bars. Dirt and dust obscured letters molded into the top of the bars. Pulling a rag from my pocket, I rubbed the top of a bar and removed the dirt so I could read the printing. The printing was strange, mostly just letters X's, V's and I's, but on the end of the bar was molded the image of a crown. Holding the light closer, I rubbed harder, and the bar began to turn gold.

Small gold coins were valuable and used as currency. Many were left over from when the Spanish ruled the territory. I could see these bars were of the same metal. I quickly pulled the cloth from other shelves. Each shelf was stacked in gold bars, some large and some small. I had never seen so much gold.

Moving around the room, I continued to pull sail cloth from the shelves revealing more stacks of gold bars. Two shelves held wooden boxes, but the shelf above hampered my attempt to raise the lids. Mustering all my strength, I pulled and tugged at the wrought iron handles, scooting one of the boxes until it teetered precariously on the edge. Toppling from the shelf, the old wooden box shattered, spilling its contents across the stones.

Treasure, pirate's treasure—I could scarcely believe my eyes. Jewelry, the likes of which I had never seen, lay spread across the floor. The meager flame of the lantern now illuminated the chamber in a multitude of colors as the light passed through a thousand gems, their little lights dancing on the ceiling and walls as I moved the lantern about.

Picking up a small crown, I placed it on my head, but it was heavy and made me teeter, so I took it off. Necklaces, bracelets, and earrings of gold and silver adorned with pearls and stones of every color lay at my feet. I thought at the time how much fun my friends and I would have playing with these shiny baubles.

Strange looking guns and swords lay across sail cloth that covered some of the gold. Standing on a lower shelf, I struggled with one hand to remove the canvas from an upper shelf.

Climbing back up with the lantern in hand, I nearly fell when I found myself staring into the darkened eyes of a skull. The skeleton of a man in a fancy, dress uniform held a saber as though he guarded the chamber. Perhaps this was the pirate himself.

With the lantern in one hand and holding on with the other, I shuffled my feet along the lower shelf. I stopped when I reached a thin shaft protruding out into the room. Still holding the lantern bail, I reached out with one finger and wiggled the shaft. That's when I recognized the shaft was the same as those I had pulled from Hickory's back. The arrow was lodged deep in the pirate's leg bone. I speculated that although he may have been alive when placed upon the shelf, it was the arrow that eventually claimed the pirate's life.

Placed here by his friends, it became his tomb. Having never returned to claim the treasure, I can only guess at the fate of those who finished sealing the chamber.

It suddenly occurred to me I might have stayed too long. My father would be furious if I were not at Blood's to meet him by seven. I dropped everything and made my way back to the surface. I covered the hole with some old board and brush I found lying strewn about the area.

Fearing I was late, I ran all the way, arriving around six thirty just as a steam boat whistle signaled the arrival of my father. Excited about my discovery, I pondered whether or not to tell him. Great riches were my father's dream, not mine. Would knowing bring us closer together, or would he simply take the gold and abandon me. I decided to contain my excitement and keep quiet until I had more time to think.

Father arrived and signaled to me from just down the street to follow him. I thought we'd be heading for the skiff to return to the *Albany*, but he was walking in the opposite direction. I finally caught up with him as we approached the Live Oak Grove.

"What are we doing here, Father? I asked.

Struggling for an answer, he said, "The skiff broke loose, and a man told me it floated down here." He scowled.

"But how do you know it's our skiff? We walked to town this morning. Shouldn't our skiff still be back where we keep the mules or at the *Albany*?"

"No! Like I said, it broke loose and floated down here. You callin' your paw a liar?"

"No, Father. I just don't understand how you could know for certain, having been gone all day," I said. After that, I kept quiet.

Down near the Live Oak Grove, we wandered out through the marsh grass, wading into the shallows. A maze of animal trails and gator slides cut through the tall grass. I puzzled how my father knew exactly what trails to take to arrive at the skiff where it sat tied to an old stump. Why was the skiff even there? Nearly a half mile south of town, we never had reason to take it out into the bay, and I found no sign that it had broken loose in the first place.

I boarded the skiff, and Father pulled us out to deeper water. He rowed us back up river to Scipio Creek where the current wasn't as strong as the river. Stepping out onto the bowery dock, he pointed at me.

"Pearl, you take the skiff and head on back to the *Albany*. I'm goin' over to Blood's and will be along later," he explained.

"Basher and Bella are dead father," I told him.

In an impatient voice, he said, "Yeah, I know all about it. Now get goin' on home, and wait for me there. Think you can do that without arguin' with me?"

I made no reply. Standing on the seat of the skiff, I pulled on the oars and rowed toward home. The skiff was not as easy to row and maneuver as the dinghy. I knew by the sun I would have to row hard to arrive before dark, and by that time, I would be worn out.

Chapter VI

Nothin' but Gator Dung

I was truly spent when the hull of the skiff slid onto the stern of the *Albany*. I was glad to be home. I lit a lantern and sat on the side of the skiff to rest. I knew I wouldn't be sitting there very long because the sun was just a glow on the horizon, and the skeeters were rising to feed.

Heading for the bow, I was almost to the stairs when I heard what sounded like a boat landing on the stern. I looked, but there was no other light, just my own lantern. I turned and made my way back, holding the lantern high, trying to find the source of the noise.

I was surprised to find a second skiff pulled up beside mine. I looked around but saw no one. I started to walk over for a closer look when I noticed wet footprints trailing from the skiff past me into the darkness of the *Albany*'s lower deck. As I turned and raised my eyes, I could see a man approaching from out of the shadows.

I couldn't see his left hand but could tell he concealed something in his right hand, keeping it tight to his body, just behind his leg. I quickly sat the lantern on the bow of the skiff and pulled my jackknife from my trouser pocket, opening it behind my back.

"Who are you, and what you want?" I yelled.

"Why they ain't no need for you be worrin'. It just come up dark all of a sudden, and I just lookin' for a place to spend the night. Why I didn't even knowed you was here girly. Is you pap here? I knowed your old pappy."

He kept talking and moving until we both stood facing each other nearest the channel. With the lantern to my back, I could see him, but he had trouble seeing me. That's when I told him.

"You're a no-good liar 'cause I know you could see me carrying that lantern. Why don't you just let me get in my boat, and I'll leave? You can take anything you want." I told him.

"The problem with that is if you leave, it means I done lost what I come for," and he slowly revealed the knife he held in his right hand.

Holding my jackknife, I held my ground. I knew he would catch me if I made a run for the bow and tried to escape through the woods. If I jumped into the channel, he would just fish me out from his boat.

I could smell his stench as he approached, sniggering under his breath. I stabbed at him with my knife, but it didn't seem to worry him much. It was when he raised his knife that I noticed the handle. It was Basher's knife, the one he kept under the bar. In a rage, I ran at him stabbing him in the leg as I passed. Screaming out in pain, he pulled the knife from his leg.

Still raging, I screamed out, "You bastard! You bastard! You killed Basher and Bella! That's Basher's knife; you killed them."

"You crazy child, I ain't kilt nobody yet. You crazy girl," he screamed back.

Limping forward, he raised his knife over me. I huddled on the deck ready to die.

Suddenly, the channel erupted as a massive wave exploded, rising high into the air over the stern. A dark form began to appear from out of the wave. I covered my head as it came crashing down, crushing my murderous pursuer into the planks. The *Albany* shook as a great weight fell upon her deck. That's when I heard a familiar sound, a drone, deeper than the lowest note of the Trinity pipes. It was a mournful sound, but now, instead of fear and misfortune, it evoked a feeling of joy and relief.

When I lowered my arms, I found myself looking into Hickory's eye. Reaching out, I rubbed his snout. Turning his head to one side, he locked his jaws onto the man's legs and pulled him screaming into the channel.

The impact knocked the lantern onto the deck, cracking the globe but not breaking it. The wick was still glowing and reignited when I picked it up.

The deck was red with blood where Hickory crushed and dragged the man into the water. With my heart pounding, I pushed at the man's boat, setting it adrift. I wanted no part of him to remain. Retrieving Basher's knife from the deck, I looked out over the water and thanked Hickory for saving my life. I turned, breathed a sigh of relief, and went to bed.

***

Early the next morning, I heard movement on the lower deck. Slipping quietly back on the upper deck, I lay down and peeked over the side to the stern. For a few minutes, it was quiet. I watched as two small gators laid sunning themselves on the blood-stained deck. As father approached, they hastily shot into the water.

Father stooped over and began inspecting the blood-soaked planks. Standing, he once again disappeared, returning moments later with his travel bags. Throwing the bags into the skiff, he pushed off and rowed toward town. I rolled over onto my back, and for a while, I tried to figure out what had just happened. *If the dead man was telling the truth and hadn't killed Bella, who did, and why was he carrying Basher's knife?*

***

Slipping into my trousers, I boarded the dinghy and headed to town. Miss Charity was pleased to see me and told me so as she helped me dress. I told her about my encounter with the man and how Hickory saved my life. Crying, she hugged me and patting my cheeks told me, "Don't never forget that you has been special blessed by God his self. You alive 'cause God got a special purpose for your life."

"What is my purpose Miss Charity?" I asked.

"God is all knowin' and do things in his own time and in his own way, and he ain't ready to tell you your purpose yet. But when God ready, you'll know, and Miss Charity can't think of nobody better than you to carry out His will. Miss Pearl, I want you to 'member, I'll always be here to help you anyway I can."

I gave Miss Charity my biggest hug and kissed her on the cheek. Running from the cabin, I headed down to see Miss Caroline.

As I approached the Florida Boarding House, I could see Miss Caroline sitting out on the porch swing. Something dreadful must have happened because Miss Caroline was holding her face in her hands weeping bitterly. Lottie and Ava knelt in front of her, crying themselves, trying to console her. I quickened my pace to see if I could help.

I ran up the steps onto the porch yelling, "Miss Caroline, Miss Caroline, what's the matter?" She took one look at me and fell from the swing onto her knees trembling, calling out my name. I ran into her arms, asking what was wrong and if I could help. She kissed me over and over again. Lottie and Ava were beside themselves and looked at me as though I was a ghost.

"Praise God, you're alive. They told me you were dead. I couldn't bear to lose you," Miss Caroline cried.

Word was spreading around town that I was murdered by the same man who killed Basher and Bella.

"The Vicar, does he think I'm dead?" I asked.

Miss Caroline released me and pointed toward the Trinity Church saying, "Yes; he brought us the news from your father. Run over and show him you're alive, and you be sure to come right back. Do you hear me, Pearl? You come right back."

I assured Miss Caroline I would return. The Trinity sat two blocks away, and I ran as fast as I could. Entering the foyer, I remembered the Vicar told me not to run in the sanctuary, so from there on, I just walked real fast. I could see the Vicar knelt down in the front of the church under the big cross, swaying and lamenting. Putting my hand on his shoulder, I asked, "Vicar are you upset 'cause of me bein' dead? 'Cause I'm okay." Turned out it was exactly why he was upset.

The Vicar was worse than Miss Caroline when it came to carrying on about me being alive. I told him what happened, and he kept interrupting saying, "Praise the Lord; praise the Lord."

I told him I didn't see the Lord there and felt Hickory deserved most of the credit.

Turns out, after reporting the tragic news, my grief-stricken father left town within the hour. It occurred to me that this could be a blessing in disguise, that I may now be free of him. But what I didn't know is a rider was dispatched to find him and deliver the good news. For the next week, between the Vicar, Miss Charity, and Miss Caroline, I was never out of their sight.

I told the Marshal I'd never seen the man before and that after our exchange of words on the *Albany,* I didn't believe he was the man who killed Basher and Bella, but because he carried Basher's knife, the Marshal was satisfied the killer was dead.

I could tell Constable Foley felt different. I stood outside the door and heard him and the Marshal having words. I waited outside in the street until Constable Foley left, slamming the door behind him. He walked out carrying Basher's hickory club in his right hand. Walking over, I handed him Basher's knife, "He'da wanted you to have this," I told him.

I decided that for now I'd just keep the gold a secret until I figured out what God had in store for me. Later in the day, I walked with Miss Caroline to an office downtown. I sat in the hall as she visited a solicitor and a Circuit Court Judge asking questions about me; she didn't seem very happy with the answers.

***

Sleep is a waking dream to a mind plagued with thoughts, and tonight my thoughts were of change. I pondered if my friends never thought of death, why was I raised to dwell upon its presence? This had to change. As if in a dream, I began thinking how I might make a family. As much as I loved Miss Charity, because she was a slave, she lived a life of limited choices. I was lucky Miss Sadie enjoyed my company and tolerated the time I spent with her slave.

On the other hand, Miss Caroline was a perfect choice for my mother, and I knew she loved me deeply, but there was a problem. Earlier in the day, sitting near a keyhole, I accidentally overheard the solicitors say that even if father abandoned me, without a husband, Miss Caroline could never be my mother.

The solution became clear. Miss Caroline needed my help to find a husband.

Miss Charity once told me, "It's best to fall asleep on a pleasant thought." I tried to hold Miss Caroline in my thoughts, but just as I was drifting off, an image of Bella with her throat slit, flashed into my mind. In that moment, any hope for sleep vanished. Filled with grief, the tears rolled from my eyes, and I began dwelling on what may have really happened.

By my accounts, none of the sums tallied. The killer was puzzled and hesitated when I identified Basher's knife and accused him of murder—murders he quickly denied.

Why was the skiff down river in the Live Oak Grove, and how did my father, who was away all day, know where to find it? It occurred to me. *The mouth of the river, what a perfect place to dump a body on an outgoing tide.*

Father seemed twitchy. Earlier when I told him, 'I was plannin' to move into town so I wouldn't be troublin' you no more.' What did he mean when he replied, 'don't be frettin' about that; I have done took care of that.'

What was it he had taken care of? What was this curse Mother placed on him that he would have to kill me rather than just allow me to leave? Would my death be Etta's insurance against my ever returning and assuming my mother's power and position in the family?

Why didn't father call out my name when he saw the blood? Why did he just assume it was mine? Father was always getting into bar fights, but no one ever died. Should I even be suspecting my father of murdering Basher and Bella?

Instead of rowing me home, did he stay in town for an alibi? Was the knife used as a partial payment for killing me, and when the killer returned to town for further payment, would father have accused him of the murders pointing to the knife as proof? I heard the clock strike four; exhausted, I finally fell asleep.

***

A week came and went before I received word of my father. Arriving back, he headed straight to the Trinity Church to confront the Vicar and demand my return. Everyone was crying as I packed and walked away, but I knew in a few months I would be back. I just needed to keep my head down and use the time wisely, making plans for my new family.

The dinghy was where I left it, and I was soon back on the *Albany*. I sat with my feet dangling over the edge of the upper deck, looking down at the bow as my father came walking through the woods.

"Understand you lucky to be alive girl. I's sure broke up when I thought you was dead.... Say, I'd surely like to see the knife that fella was totin'. What ever happened to that knife?"

"I give it to Constable Foley," I said.

"More'n likely for the best I reckon. You think they's any chance that fella could still be alive out there?" he nervously asked.

He was more concerned with the whereabouts of the knife and the killer than he was of me.

"No, I don't reckon so. Old Hickory damn near broke him in half for' draggin' him under. I figure by now, that killer, he ain't nothin' but gator dung." Looking down at my feet, I hesitated then suggested to him, "You know something; if'n I was you, I'd stay back from that water. Hickory don't seem to take kindly to folks who don't care for me.... I got lots of friends feel that way."

When I looked back, he was white as a sheet. The question I asked myself was, *could my father have hired this man to kill me?*

"Passions of love and hate hold boundless powers, virtuous and wicked, able to alter the best intentions of men. Many fail to control them and are consumed by their passing, but love and hate weight only one end of the scale; the other holds a great evil—indifference." Pearl

Chapter VII

Coming to Grips

June of 1859 marked the close of cotton shipping season in Apalachicola but the beginning of cotton harvest up-river. Father secured passage on the packet steamer *Chewala* to carry the wagon and mules up the Apalachicola and Flint Rivers to Bainbridge, Georgia. Here we would stay until November, and father would work hauling freight.

He hoped to find work with one of the steamship companies, either Thronateeska Navigation or the Callahan Lines. If not between the turpentine camps, two cotton factories, and the plantations, a man with mules and a dray could make an honest living.

Southern plantations would soon bustle as millions of slaves picked, ginned, baled, and stored the cotton to await shipment. It would be November before church congregations would begin praying for the rains of December. High water was needed, so steamers laden with cotton could navigate down the river to Apalachicola where the shipping season would begin again.

An ominous feeling now fell upon me. This would be the longest five months of my life as I awaited passage back to my beloved Apalachicola.

Distraught over my father's behavior—once aboard *Chewala* I hid out, trying my best to avoid him. Finding a quiet bench in front of the Pilot house, I occupied my time by scrutinizing the powerful steamer as she pushed her way up-stream.

It was not long before I resolved that even a mighty boat like *Chewala* was a slave and no freer than the Negroes forced to stoke her boilers. Held captive by the land on a watery chain, she was forced by the hand of the same master to wander through the wilderness allowing commerce to connect our commercial centers.

Mesmerized in thought, at times it felt as though the waters of the river flowed through me, and we became as one. I found solace on this river, and it wrapped me like a warm blanket on a cold night.

Artistic Rendition of *The River Bride*

On shore, the only signs of life were an occasional landing or a cabin tucked away on a forested bluff. In the distance, I heard the whistle of the *River Bride*; like the *Chewala,* she carried a shallow draft and was one of the steamers that could still navigate when the river was so shallow. She would soon pass by heading downstream. Oh, how I wished I were on the *River Bride*, heading south, toward home.

It wasn't long before I envisioned myself a stowaway, traveling up-river, making my way deep into Georgia, to Atlanta, where I would start a new life, and my father would never think to look.

It was with a whistle and bell the great steamboats found voice. In a language all their own, they called out to one another as they plied the river basin. When a steam whistle sounded somewhere, a flurry of activity commenced.

From miles around, cargo arrived at landings, and people gathered to greet seldom seen relatives. Warehouse doors opened, and slaves congregated to relieve the massive steamboats of their burdens. Cotton, barrels of rosin, goods of all description rolled down ramps and were stacked in warehouses to await sale.

A ship's bell commanded a crew as well as a spoken word, sending men scurrying to duty. The sound of the bell announced a dignitary coming aboard, warned of low water and snags, and in a fog, it cried out, "We are here; we are here." Twice an hour it would ring, no need for a clock for everyone knew, "Eight bells and all is well." At midnight on New Year's Eve, it would strike the most, sixteen bells, eight for the old and eight for the new. But once in a while, if a little girl was very good, under the watchful eye of the captain, this good little girl could ring that bell and assume her first command.

When I was very young, I sought father's attentions. I suppose it is in every child to seek the sanction of a parent. Never receiving the attention I craved, I was forced to look elsewhere, sometimes taking love from the most unlikely of places. Slaves locked away in hot boxes or held in chains seemed to hold no malice toward me. I often spoke to them and listened as they prayed to God for deliverance.

Same God? I puzzled why they were praying to a white God. A preacher once told me that God created man in his own image, and by virtue of this, God was white. I remember one night listening at the flap of a revival tent. I heard another preacher say that no one has ever looked upon the face of God, and so I asked myself, how would anyone know his color?

If god created man in his own image, why did he make them in so many colors? It became obvious to me that when it came to making men, God didn't care about color and accepted them no matter what color he pooped out.

Color, religion, or politics, my father could find a reason to hate most men, but for some reason, the same rules didn't apply to women. My father was never discrete, and I knew what it was for a man to lay with a woman. I'd witnessed him laying with any woman that would have him or that he could afford, no matter their color.

***

Two types of steamboats navigated the river system, the sternwheeler and the sidewheeler. Most frequent were the sidewheelers, being more maneuverable on a meandering river system, but because of the weight distribution of the engines, a sternwheeler could carry massive loads. By 1890, for reasons unknown, sidewheelers all but disappeared.

The two types were then broken down into six categories according to purpose.

First, the Packets, long-range steamers plying the river and carrying cargo, passengers, and mail, built long and wide, they carried a shallow draft even under the heaviest loads; at the same time, the upper decks offered nice accommodation for those who could pay. For those without much money, the lower deck offered cramped accommodations next to the livestock. During the cotton shipping season, it was all about profit, and the packets were seen traveling down river looking like giant bales of cotton.

Towboats, small and powerful, pushed barges up and down the river. Leaving empty barges for loading, they picked up barges of raw material for processing and then carried the finished product down river to market.

Ferries simply transported passengers across the rivers. Ferries were usually identified by the name of the landings they serviced.

Fuelers carried wood and coal from the shore to the steamer, allowing them to refuel in route, thereby keeping the commerce flowing.

Few in number were the massive snag boats; most were controlled by the government. Respected and supported by all, they traveled the river system looking for submerged logs and snags left by storms. Using an enormous boom protruding from the bow, they would hoist the obstruction from the river, making it safe for all to pass.

Showboats were the most elusive. I never saw one on the Apalachicola River. Those palaces were reserved for big rivers like the Mississippi and seldom ventured elsewhere.

I loved these old steamboats, and over the years, like my heart and soul, they became a part of me. But times changed, and the rivers, once the only passage to the Gulf of Mexico were being replaced by iron rails and steam locomotives.

To me, trains were an abomination as they cut their way east to west across the face of the country. To my mind, they were thieves, stealing our livelihood by eliminating the need for a river. Instead of water, the rails now carried the cotton straight to the Atlantic Ocean where it would find passage to New York and Europe. Soon it would be the railroad that would own and control the remaining steamboats.

On this journey, I dwelt on thoughts that should never have occurred to a child, thoughts reserved for older minds. Like Yellow fever, the rumors of war had found safe harbor in the South since before I was born. Fueled by half-truths, the threat finally reached that terrifying place beyond diplomacy—war.

My mind carried me back to an old memory where I stood on a street outside a bar in Pensacola, and a man entertained his friends by reading from a newspaper. He said the story was about a speech that some damn, old, black woman up in Ohio made back in fifty-one.

With all the unrest brewing up between the North and the South, I'm sure reprinting the story sold even more papers.

He went on to say that evidently, them damn Yankees let this black woman give a speech, and as if letting her talk wasn't bad enough, during her talk, she rebuked a white man. "Den dat little man in back dar, he say women can't have as much rights as men 'cause Christ wasn't a woman! Whar did your Christ come from? Whar did your Christ come from? From God and women! Man had nothin' to do wid Him."

The gathered men became outraged that this old nigger woman was allowed to speak in the first place, and for a nigger woman to rebuke a white was an unforgivable sin. I did not share in their anger. Confused, I began to pity these men, for in their rage, they were blinded by hate. The content of her words had fallen on deaf ears.

I was very young and didn't understand all of what was said at the time, but I remembered the words, and they sounded to me like a truth—probably how she got her name, Miss Truth, Miss Sojourner Truth.

***

Sunset found my father busying himself by drinking and gambling on the lower deck. To my surprise, the Captain came and joined me on my bench. He was very curious what a little girl could possibly be thinking to have kept her still, sitting on a bench, all day long. We were having the most wonderful conversation when two stewards interrupted, one carrying a small table and the other carrying the Captain's supper.

The smell of the food made me realize I had not eaten all day. I started to leave when the Captain invited me to dine with him. When I saw two plates, I graciously accepted his invitation.

Captain Berry said we shouldn't stand on ceremony and just tuck in. That was fine by me; I didn't know what the ceremony was anyway, and I was just about starved to death.

I slept on the back of the dray using my bag as a pillow. The skeeters weren't bad; they never seemed to fly very far from shore. I always figured they couldn't swim, and the moving water made them nervous.

I was awakened when the *Chewala* whistled signaling our arrival in Bainbridge. I woke up a bit cranky because of a crick in my neck. I was sure missing my feather bed back at Miss Caroline's. The stewards passed by and did not see me in the shadows. One said to the other, "Poor little thing, she ain't got a chance." I can remember feeling bad for whomever they were talking about.

I thought a good stretch might put everything in order, but as I breathed in heavy, I started smellin' somethin' kinda' ripe. Turns out it was me.

Before Miss Charity and Miss Sadie, if you da told me I'd ever want to willingly take a bath, I'd of said you was crazy. But smellin' the way I did and after lookin' in the river at my reflection, with my hair all tangled up, I knew for certain I needed a bath and a brush; even my teeth felt like they were covered in fur.

Miss Caroline was kind enough to have packed me a small bag with what she called, "a lady's essentials." I decided I'd better take a look. Inside, there was a brush and comb, two bars of soap, and a brand-new badger hair toothbrush that had come all the way from Europe. I couldn't believe after all these years a little bit of dirt could make me feel so uncomfortable and self-conscious. I even thought I should unpack a dress because I didn't feel comfortable wearing my favorite trousers anymore.

***

When in Bainbridge, we stayed in an abandoned shack just north of the stock pens. It was tolerable except when the wind blew from the south. After passing over the stock pens, the odor could take your breath away. Father liked it because he could keep the mules close. The grazing was good, and he could steal enough hay and grain from the stock yard to supplement the mule's feed.

I heard the wagon pull out early the next morning. Father left me a few coins on the stand next to the door to buy food. I wasn't all that hungry, so I made do with a couple of spoons of beans left over in the pot from the night before, along with a heel of bread.

Irritated by a few flea bites on my arms and legs, I threw my bedding out over the hitching post, hoping a dog might walk by and the fleas would prefer the dog to my blanket.

Our water came from a spring fed creek just behind the shack. It was just a short walk, maybe a quarter mile to the spring itself, and to me, the spring was the most wondrous of places. The water of the spring stayed the same temperature no matter the season. Rock shelves fell into the water like steps before dropping off into a deep blue hole. I could escape the hot sun in the shade of a live oak tree or lay on rock ledges and bask in its warmth.

I sat for a while with my feet dangling in the water, taking it all in before beginning my ablutions. I washed my clothes first and laid them in the sun on the hot rocks to dry. Taking a rag in hand, I began scrubbing myself. Without Miss Charity's help, I was careful to wash everything, even parts no one could see, and soon the soap was carrying my dirt and grime down the creek.

After a thorough cleaning, all that was left was my hair, and I knew without help, it was a day's project. I battled it with comb and brush for a good half hour, making little progress.

Suddenly, a blood curdling war whoop sent chills down my spine and woodland creatures scurrying for cover. Expecting an attack, I turned just in time to see a slip of a boy leap naked from the highest rock ledge and splash into the springs. I doubted he could have been much more than three or four, but he could swim like a fish. He finally came up for a breath, and I was ready to ask what he was doing here all by himself when a young girl about my age walked out of the wood and onto the rocks.

Speaking in broken English, I could tell she was apologizing for her brother's behavior. Then, in a stern voice "Zelig Freud, you must behave," she shouted. Zelig disappeared back under the water, unwilling to listen, acting as though he hadn't heard her at all. I shook my head and smiled at her. I knew this was a woman's way of saying: I understand—men are all alike.

She approached down the rock steps and signaling with her hand, made a gesture as though brushing her hair. I handed her my brush and comb, and she began to tame my tangles. "Odila," she spoke, smiling, pointing at herself with the comb.

"Pearl," I said, returning her smile.

Odila's hair was a beautiful, honey blonde with long curls falling down to her shoulders. We soon agreed I would help her learn better English, and she would teach me some words in German and help me with my hair.

It was two years since Odila, Zelig, and their parents moved from Germany to Columbus, Georgia where Mr. Freud joined his brother in business, Freud Millwork Supply.

The brothers were experts in the production of fabrics and supplied equipment, parts, and expertise necessary in the running of spinning and weaving mills. Two fabric mills were up and running near Bainbridge, and they decided to open a branch store to supply the mills. The brothers had a good reputation in Columbus and were known for being fair and honest in all their dealings, a prerequisite for doing business with Ira Sanborn. You couldn't throw a rock in Decatur County, Georgia without hitting a Sanborn property.

Sanborn, an early pioneer, made his way up the Apalachicola and Flint rivers, spending a few years in Apalachicola and Quincy, Florida before finally settling in Decatur County, Georgia on the Attapulgus Creek near Bainbridge. Here, Ira would harness the rivers to power his enterprises.

Ira W. Sanborn owned a tannery, a shoe and harness factory, a gristmill, a sawmill, a cigar factory, and a mercantile store. In 1856, he built the Estahatchee Mill and began producing Kersey, a fabric made of a cotton and wool blend. It was a good fabric but made me itch. I always figured God must have been mad at sheep 'cause he gave them wool coats.

Ira Sanborn

Thanks to Odila, my hair now hung in a loose braid to the center of my back. I thanked her, stroking the braid, admiring it in the reflection of the spring.

Zelig disappeared from view but not from ear shot. We could hear him cracking rocks not too far away. He soon appeared with a variety of colored, chalk rock, cradling the stones in his arms, being careful not to drop any. Odila, patting Zelig's head, commended him on his selection. I puzzled what they were up to, but soon Odila began to use the soft rock to draw on the flat ledges.

Odila was an artist. I could not believe my eyes when creatures and landscapes began to emerge from the soft stone she held in her hand. She smiled, handing me a few of the chalk rocks, insisting I sit and draw on the stone beside her. Her talent was awe-inspiring; even the young Zelig was showing an aptitude for describing the world in pictures. Intimidated by her talent, I sat watching, but once again, she began pointing to the stone and encouraged me to draw.

I decided to draw an old friend, and soon a rough image of Hickory began to appear. I wanted him to look real, like Odila's images, but it came out more like a picture in the newspaper used to make fun of some politician. All finished, we stood looking at each other's drawings. Zelig chuckled when he looked at Hickory, and I blushed in embarrassment. Odila poked Zelig in the shoulder and told him not to be cruel, and she thought it was very good.

"Do you know this creature?" Odila asked.

"Very well. He's a good friend of mine, and one night not so long ago, he saved my life."

Zelig stood with a curious but skeptical look on his face, and an excited Odila began prompting me to tell the story, so not wanting to disappoint after my dismal failure as an artist, I sat down on the ledge just above them and began telling them of my encounters with Old Hickory.

They both sat mesmerized as I told the tale of how I freed Hickory. With my jackknife in hand, I pretended to cut at the snare lines, describing the sound of the net as it slid into the channel. Zelig flinched when, straining with all my might, I began pulling arrows from the back of the great beast. Odila's eyes were as big as saucers as an evil man approached from out of the darkness wielding Basher's knife. I showed them how I ran at him screaming, burying my jackknife deep into his leg.

Crouching down, I covered my eyes, preparing to die as Basher's knife was raised and made ready for a death blow. Odila's hands were trembling; when playing the part of Hickory, I exploded into the air quickly, falling down and crushing the assassin into the deck of the *Albany*. A clap of my hands became the thunderous snap of his jaws as Hickory, holding tight, dragged the killer screaming into the dark water. Zelig, now a believer, looked over his shoulder into the spring, checking for movement beneath the water. When I finished, they cheered and clapped as though I was an actor on a stage.

Excited, Odila stated, "You are a wonderful story teller. How can you make up such an extraordinary tale just in your head? I could never imagine such a story in my head."

I assured them that it was not a tall tale, and my story was in fact true.

"But these terrible things you speak could not happen to a child?" With great empathy, Odila reached out and held my hand.

Looking at Odila in that moment reminded me of Bella, and I began weeping bitterly and soon we were all crying, even Zelig. Odila was afraid she had said something to offend and upset me and was asking for forgiveness. I calmed myself and assured her that she was not the cause of my grief. I told her I once had a special friend named Bella but could not finish my thought as the tears once again welled up inside me.

"This special friend Bella, would it be good for you to speak of her? I will listen," Odila offered.

"No, I cannot. There are some stories I hold within me that God has not yet created enough words to tell. Sometimes I feel as though if I were to tell the story of my friend, at the end, I would die of my own sorrow.

Chapter VIII

Suspect

    Odila, feeling my pain, was kind enough to change the subject. Zelig rushed to the highest ledge and raised our spirits by doing flips into the spring. I believe Odila was just as pleased as I to have found a new friend. She invited me to their house where all morning, her mother had prepared her famous meat pies for dinner. Odila helped me button my dress, and we headed to town.

    You could have found the Freud home from a block away just by following the wonderful smell of the meat pies baking in the oven. Odila's mother, Ida, spoke with the same broken English, but after a generous hug and having my cheeks pinched, I knew I was a part of the family. I didn't think the pies could ever taste as good as they smelled, but I was wrong. Miss Ida excused Mr. Freud's absence by stating the fact that only Mr. Sanborn at the Estahatchee Mill could have kept him away from his favorite meat pies.

    Having had only a couple of spoons of beans for my breakfast, I was starved, but after scarfing down a dinner of three meat pies, I felt like a tick ready to burst. I knew they'd easily hold me till morning; this way I wouldn't have to worry about finding supper that night.

    Mr. Freud returned home midday, and Odila and Zelig ran to meet him. Mr. Freud grabbed each, hoisted them into the air and gave each a hug and kiss, all the time calling them his little *Lieblings*. Turning to me, he stood tall and asked, "Momma, has the stork brought us another child while I was away?"

"No, no, this is good friend. Her name is Pearl," Miss Ida replied.

Seeing a look in his eyes, I started to flee, but he grabbed me and tossed me into the air shouting, "Three *Lieblings* is much better than just two." He kissed me on the cheek and gave me a hug. Odila and Zelig were laughing out loud at the stunned look on my face.

Grabbing Miss Ida, he danced around the room. "Break out the cherry cordial for the children and the wine for us Momma. We sold the new machines to Mr. Sanborn. We must celebrate," he shouted.

Even full of meat pies, I was still able to find room for cookies and cherry cordial. I couldn't understand the conversation when it would drift into German, but I didn't have to speak the language to sense the excitement and join in the celebration.

When it was time to leave, Odila walked me to the door. She handed me a bag her mamma had packed with two meat pies and bread. I asked Odila, "What's a *Liebling*?"

"It is a darling or a sweetheart," she said, pointing to me. "It is you Pearl. You are my *Liebling*."

She hugged me asking, "Can I visit you at your house in the morning?"

Embarrassed, I told her I lived far away, and it would be better to meet here; that way we could spend the day in town looking through all the shop windows. Excited, she agreed, and I left, headed back toward the shack.

I arrived back at the shack before father. Gathering up the blankets I had laid on the hitching rail, I carried them to the back room where I slept. I was in high spirits, looking forward to spending the day with Odila.

I grabbed an old broom and began sweeping, tidying up. I knew it wouldn't make much difference; in this shack, a broom was a poor substitute for a match. I was really just hoping it would wear me out, so I would have no choice but to sleep tonight.

Father arrived back with the dray and mules a little after dark, but he wasn't alone. Standing back from the open door, concealed in shadows, I could see he was followed by two men on horseback and two more on foot, carrying torches. While they were busy with the animals, I slipped up and quietly latched the door.

I knew it would be a long night. They had started early and already smelled of whiskey. A fire was started in the pit out front, and an old Indian blanket was spread on the ground. Hanging a lantern on a branch above the blanket, they broke out the cards, dice, and a couple of jugs of shine.

From what I could hear, they had partnered up on a job to move equipment from Bainbridge to the cotton mill. They kept talking about some haughty foreman of Old Man Sanborn's who instructed them on handling the delicate machines to insure their safe arrival to the mill.

To hear them talking, they were never once grateful for a good paying job. They just seemed envious of Sanborn's money and resentful of anyone telling them what to do. The more they drank, the louder and more insufferable they became. It was after midnight before they passed out around the fire.

It was early morning, still dark, when I heard someone outside my window. Most of the glass in the window was missing, so to remain hidden, I didn't dare even breathe. It was hard to remain silent; he stunk so badly, I could feel myself wanting to gag. I heard him pissing on the boards of the shack under the window. In a quiet, low voice, he spoke.

"You in there girly? I know you is. I's can smell you, and you smell real purdy…. Why don't you come on out here and help me put my pecker away?"

I could smell his breath as he peered through the broken glass, trying to get a look at me. Suddenly, the silence was broken when from out by the fire, my drunken father called out. "Where the hell are you? You bastard! Aldridge! You God damn better not be going through my things. You steal from me, I'll gut you like a fish, boy."

Aldridge quickly moved back around to the side of the shack.

"I's just takin' a piss. Can't a man take a piss 'round here without bein' gutted," Aldridge hollered back.

"Best you stay out here by the fire. You can take a piss somewhere else," father scolded, before passing out again.

Too frightened to sleep, I gathered my things and waited until I was sure they were asleep. I slowly slipped out by the fire and gathered the money left lying on the blanket and carefully pulled the watch from Aldridge's vest pocket. I figured he owed me for being an ass. If I were lucky, they'd wake up, accuse each other, and gut one another.

A sliver of a moon offered enough light that I could make my way up the stream to the spring where I hoped to get a couple of hours of sleep before daybreak. I covered myself with lace and gauze fabric to keep the mosquitos at bay and soon fell asleep on a cool rock ledge.

***

The sun was just lighting the horizon when I woke with a troubled mind. It wasn't fair. He didn't even check on me, and he could care less if I were alive or dead. While Aldridge threatened me, his only concern was for a few meager possessions he seemed to treasure. I had received warmer greetings from total strangers than from my own father. It shouldn't have to be this way. It was painful to realize that I lived a life outside the rules that governed civilized people.

I guess I should be grateful I didn't feel this way more often. I always felt selfish when I'd sit around feeling sorry for myself. I knew it was a sin asking God to simply take me away rather than having my friends discover the truth of my life. My salvation was the plan I had been forming in my mind. If I wanted a different life, I needed to make it happen. The sooner we returned to Apalachicola, the better. I pulled myself up, dressed, and headed to town.

My first stop was the pawnbroker to sell the watch. I had to sell it here—brokers didn't ask questions. I would have to be very shrewd to get a good price. I knew the Vicar would not approve. He believed that too many times being shrewd bordered on lying.

The broker stood and greeted me from behind the counter as I walked through the door. He seemed nice enough, so I walked over and laid the watch on the counter. "Good morning, sir. My father asked me to stop by and see if you would make an offer on his watch."

"Is your father with you?" he inquired.

"No. He's out looking for work. I just hate to think of him selling my grandfather's watch, but he told me times are hard, and taking care of me was more important than any family heirloom," I said, as if relaying my father's true feelings. After hearing the words leave my mouth, I had an epiphany of what the Vicar was talking about, but this was one time, the devil at my elbow would have to win the argument. I needed the money for passage.

Examining the watch, the broker asked, "How much is your father asking for the watch?"

"I don't know. Father said I was to let you make an offer. Then, I'm to take it over to the jewelers when he opens and let him make an offer. Father will decide tonight where I sell it," I responded. The thought of burning in hell began to weigh heavy on my mind as I crossed from shrewdness to barefaced lying. The Vicar's rules made it very hard to conduct business.

The broker continued to examine the watch, opening compartments I didn't know existed. His eyes lit up when the watch began to chime, but when it started playing music like a musical box, he quickly closed the case. In that moment, I wanted to take the watch back, but because of my lies, I had to continue my facade as though I knew the watch played music all along.

"I'll tell you what I'll do, young Miss. I'll save you a trip to the jewelers and give you top dollar here and now. If tonight your father doesn't like the deal, come back tomorrow morning, and I'll exchange it back with no hard feelings. How does sixty dollars sound?" I nearly passed out.

Having had some experience with gold, I knew it was valuable. I suspected the watch was made of gold, but I was thinking perhaps a few dollars. What was a man like Aldridge doing with a watch of this quality? Who did he kill to get it? My heart was pounding as I reached out to seal our deal with a handshake. As I left the shop, I just knew that neither God nor the Vicar would be very pleased with the greedy little grin on my face.

Odila was anxiously waiting on the steps when I arrived, and she ran out to greet me. She had already bribed Zelig with the promise of sweets if he'd stay home and not tag along. I told Odila I was hungry, and she grabbed my arm and pointed me toward downtown.

As we walked, she told me about a Frenchman who opened a restaurant, and his food although *seltsam*, which turned out to be strange, was *fabelhaft* and *wunderbar,* two more new German words that I translated to mean fabulous and wonderful.

The owner met us at the door and led us to a table. Since neither of us recognized anything on the menu, I asked if he would pick something he liked, and we'd have that for breakfast. He agreed and soon returned with a *seltsam* dish. It smelled good, but I had to ask, "What is it?"

"*Crepe Ratatouille*," he exclaimed.

"Rat," I said with a worried look.

"No, not rat," we chuckled as he made a face like a mouse. "Just called rat; the name is different in French," he said, putting my mind at ease.

Along with those meat pies, it was one of the best things I ever put in my mouth. We were about finished when he showed up with something he called a *beignet*. One taste, and I just knew I had died and gone to heaven. *Beignets* were now on the top of my list. We thanked him for a *wunderbar* breakfast.

I was surprised that I didn't feel all that guilty paying for our breakfast with my ill-gotten booty.

Looking up and down the street, Odila and I made a plan so as not to miss anything. Suddenly, I was filled with a sense of dread as I spotted the back of the dray pulled in the alley beside Freud Millwork Supply. We made our way down the street, pressing our noses against display windows and weaving in and out of shops for a closer look at those items that intrigued us. I was careful to try and keep Odila between me and the dray so as not to be seen.

It wasn't long before Odila asked, "Pearl, what is wrong? Why do you keep looking around?"

"Odila, forgive me, but I saw a man down by your father's store who scares me, and I don't want him to see me." I couldn't bring myself to tell her there were actually two men, and one was my father.

Odila wanted to see the man who scared me, and so we turned it into a kind of game as we made our way down the street, hiding behind crates and barrels or ducking into shops to avoid detection.

Sanborn's Mercantile Store sat across from Freud's, and from there, I felt safe to watch Aldridge and the other men from last night loading a large machine onto the wagon. I realized the foreman they begrudged around the fire last night had to be Mr. Freud.

Turning around, I nearly fainted at the sight of my father standing over me scowling down. He was holding a length of rope he'd just purchased to secure the load. Odila, thinking it was the man I feared, held my hand and was ready to help me stand my ground.

"What you doin' here Pearl?" he asked.

"Nothing Father; just looking around with my friend is all," I responded, trembling.

"You know anything about some money and watch that come up missin'?" he asked in an accusing tone.

"No, Father," I lied.

"Where was you this mornin' girl? I called you to fetch water but couldn't find ya."

"I stayed in town last night father."

"Where did ya' stay last night?"

Odila, knowing I was scared, spoke up. "Pearl stayed with me last night, sir."

Lashing out, in a low, cruel voice Father asked, "Who the hell are you? I didn't ask you. I asked Pearl. Where did ya' stay last night girl?"

Scared out of my mind, I was speechless. That's when Odila made a bold move. "To answer your question, I am Odila Freud. That is my father's business across the street where your wagon sits. If there is a problem, I am sure we can talk to my papa and fix this problem."

The change in my father was swift, and he quickly apologized for being curt. He handed me a few coins and said I should take my friend over to the counter and buy some sweets.

He left, but I knew somehow, I would pay for this later. To have been bested by a little German girl would not bode well with my father.

I felt as though I owed Odila an explanation. Over the next few days, while father moved the machines to the mill, I shared my story and my plan with my *liebling* Odila, making her promise not to tell another living soul.

Father finished the job and went over to Freud's to collect the payment. As we walked back out to the shack, he announced he had received a good job offer and decided to return to Apalachicola. He instructed me to be at the docks first thing in the morning and to wait near the steamer called *River Bride*. Having already booked passage, we were due to depart mid-morning. Showing no emotion, I said, "Yes sir," but inside I screamed out in celebration. I thought to myself: *It must be ordained. My prayer was answered; it had to be a sign from God.* The *River Bride* was the steamer we passed traveling up to Bainbridge—the very steamer I prayed would carry me back to Apalach.

I so wanted to turn and run back to town to tell Odila the good news, but I knew better than to cross my father. The news would have to wait till morning. With over sixty dollars hidden in my petticoat and passage on the next steamer south, I was on the top of the world.

It was around midnight when I stirred to the sound of voices off in the distance. Moving into the front room, I could see torches down on the road at the end of our path. I shivered when I realized it was my father and his new-found cronies. I prayed they wouldn't come this way and was relieved when I saw them move down the road toward town. I figured he was just settling up with his partners and maybe moving the dray and mules down to the dock for the trip.

Next morning, I was up like a shot. My bags were already packed, and with no sign of my father, I was out the door heading to town. I had no intention of missing that boat.

Arriving at the dock, I found the mules and dray tied off to a hitching post. I threw my bag on the back of the wagon so father would see the bag and know I was close. There were six large barrels of rosin loaded and tied down on the wagon, so I figured he must be hauling rosin down to the boat yard near Apalach.

Running down the street, I passed the Freud Mill Work Supply. I glanced in the windows, but all was quiet. It was not quite six o'clock. There were a few shopkeepers about, but they weren't conducting business, only sweeping their porches and washing windows in preparation for the day's business.

I knew it was early, but I couldn't wait, so I knocked on Odila's door, but there was no answer. I knocked a little harder and called out her name, but there was still no response. I wandered down the street looking in the restaurant windows, hoping to find them having an early breakfast, but my search was to no avail. I decided to return to the wagon and wait until the Freud's opened for business. I was sure Mr. Freud would know where I could find Odila.

Back at the wagon, I climbed on top of the barrels for a better view of the street. Impatient, I pulled a piece of chalk rock out of my bag and began drawing on the barrel tops. I drew a picture of Hickory on the top of each barrel, and underneath the picture I wrote the words, "Gator Rosin." I chuckled to imagine people trying to figure out what could be in a barrel marked Gator Rosin.

I heard the town clock strike eight and made my way back downtown, looking for Odila, but still no luck. I was very worried that I might not get to see my friend before I left.

As I walked back to the dock, a man came running down the street and started ringing the town's alarm bell. "Fire! Fire!" He shouted, and men came scrambling out of their shops and homes to answer the alarm. "It's the Turpentine Still! There's a fire heading through the wood toward the still!" All the men of the town began hitching their wagons and gathering shovels and equipment. Cracking their whips, they raced out of town toward the still. Off in the distance, from over the tops of the buildings on the main street, I could see smoke rising into the air.

I ran fast as I could back to the wagon. It was nearly nine o'clock, and I couldn't afford to miss the boat. The town had all but closed down with everyone heading to the fire. That's when I saw my father and Aldridge coming down the street, carrying a chest draped with a blanket. I couldn't tell much about it except for the shape and size. I hid behind the barrels and felt the wagon sag as they heaved the heavy chest up just behind the driver's seat.

"We'll meet up down river for the split. You best be gettin' out of town," Father told Aldridge.

I thought it strange at the time that they wouldn't just split the money for moving the equipment here in Bainbridge. *Why meet up later?* At that moment, an explosion rocked the town. The impact shattered several shop windows, and the mules jolted forward, throwing me off the wagon to the ground in front of a wheel. Fortunately, the harness held, and the wheel stopped just short of running me over. I climbed back up on the wagon in time to see an enormous plume of smoke rising into the air from where the still had exploded. Aldridge hurried away as father grabbed the bridle and led the team down the ramp onto the *River Bride*. When he looked back at the wagon, I was sitting in my seat.

Commerce drove the river trade, and it would take far more than a local fire to bring it to a halt. Before the wagon came to rest, smoke billowed from the stacks, and the giant wheels of the *River Bride* began to turn. Filled with anticipation and a renewed hope, I watched as the *River Bride* made her way out to the main channel, heading south toward home.

My heart ached not having said goodbye to Odila. To fill the time, I decided to compose my first letter. Without writing accoutrements, I rehearsed the words in my mind and committed them to memory. I figured to buy the best paper, ink, and one of those metal dip pens when I got back to Apalach. It filled me with delight when I imagined sitting on the porch swing at the Florida Boarding House, putting my words on paper, and thinking how exciting it would be for Odila to receive a letter in the mail.

Chapter IX

Cat O' Nine Tails

We hadn't traveled far on the *River Bride* when we came across one of the many steamers that shared the popular name *Ben Franklin*. This *Ben Franklin* had run aground on the shallow river bed. Men were working frantically to transfer her cargo, trying to lighten her load. If the river continued to fall, she would soon be in her death throes, crushed beneath her own weight.

Father, now flush with money, bought his way into a poker game on the upper deck. I couldn't help but think that over the years we could have lived a good life on just the money he threw away on gambling, whiskey, and loose women.

By noon, with my letter memorized, I began to ramble about the boat. Even with the river so shallow, we were making good time. One crewman stood near the bow calling out depth and another called out speed. In some places, where the river channel flowed deep, we were making ten to twelve knots.

The cook had prepared a pot of stew for the first-class passengers and was surprised when I handed him the money for a bowl with bread. I carried it up to the bench in front of the pilot's house to eat with a view of the river. It was here I met the prettiest man I had ever seen, Captain Hatch Wefing.

He was tall and handsome with a handlebar mustache and a well-trimmed beard. Captain Wefing was training a new pilot, supervising from the bench where I was going to sit. Several of the passengers' children sat on the deck in front of the bench. He motioned me to join them.

Captain Wefing was relaying the details of a battle he had recently fought against an enormous, terrifying creature called a Kraken. I came in on the middle of his tale, but the thought of Captain Wefing with his harpoon single handedly driving the beast, with its twenty thrashing tentacles back into the ocean depths, made my encounter with Hickory seem rather plain. I tried to eat my stew, but at times, as the great battle evolved, my hand jerked, spilling the contents of my spoon back into the bowl.

I would have to keep a wary eye on Captain Wefing for the rest of our journey. Only the finest men would be added to my list of proper suitors to woo Miss Caroline. I was very encouraged to have found a suitor in such a short time. Perhaps, finding Miss Caroline a husband would be easier than I first thought.

Loaded heavily at Bainbridge, we were scheduled to make five landings before arriving at Apalachicola. Most stops boarded passengers instead of cargo, so it didn't slow us down much. The river was very low, but Captain Wefing proceeded with every confidence, navigating the river as though he could see the river bottom through the muddy water.

I followed him around, hiding in his wake to better establish his true character. I felt I was being very sly, but at times, he glanced back and smiled at me, and for some unfathomable reason, I blushed and grinned. I soon realized this power he controlled was by no means an asset. It seemed that all the ladies onboard, married or not, were also blushing and grinning. It felt as though he was cheating on Miss Caroline with his flirting ways. That is, if he had met her before.

The trip down river was going well until Father hollered my name.

Overwhelmed with a sense of trepidation, I answered, "Yeah."

We were just coming up to the Narrows, and it appeared as though we might depart just short of Apalachicola. I heard the sound of my heart dropping clear down into my shoes.

With the river so shallow, we were forced to unload the wagon well off shore. The mules, accustomed to water crossings, headed down the ramp, and with water up to their bellies, they forded the river heading to shore. Looking back over the rosin barrels, I waved goodbye to the *River Bride* and was very excited to see Captain Wefing waving back from the pilot house.

We came out onto the Apalachee Trail a few hours north of the turpentine camp. I hoped this early departure wouldn't delay us long because I knew Apalachicola lay at the end of the trail just a few hours past the camp. We were soon joined by a couple of wagons from the camp loaded with rosin. Together, we waited for a towboat and barge that would carry the barrels of rosin to the boat works along the river.

The talk amongst the waiting men was not of commerce but of preparations for war. They all believed there would soon be a boom in the demand for navel stores, that is to say, the turpentine and rosin needed to seal the hulls of wooden vessels designed for war.

Eventually, the furnaces at the Columbus Iron Works would be fired around the clock to produce the metal trappings necessary to equip new war ships along with the production of armaments needed to defend them. The Columbus textile mills needed to begin production of uniforms to dress an army.

All I knew for sure was the army was conspicuous by its absence, and the rumors of this upcoming war had been a topic of tavern talk since before I was born. Although my concern was growing, because from what I was reading in newspapers on the River Bride, those rumors were now coming from higher government sources. Father soon changed the topic with a roll of his dice, and the men began to gamble.

I wandered the shoreline with a poking stick I had selected from the edge of the trail. I could entertain myself for hours with a good poking stick, overturning stones, probing at shadows beneath the water, drawing pictures in the mud, or writing things like, "Pearl was here." The sound of a whistle in the distance ended the game of chance, and the men began making preparations to unload the barrels.

A shallow draft barge pushed by the towboat, *Little Boy*, appeared around the bend, and soon the barge was lowering its ramp onto the river bank. I was surprised when Father made a deal with the towboat pilot to take his barrels of rosin for under market price. It appeared as though he just wanted to get rid of them. I was suspicious of Father's motives and added this to my mental list of why I didn't trust him. Having lost at dice, the men on the other wagons had to unload Father's barrels and roll them on to the barge to pay their debt.

With the barrels unloaded, we climbed aboard the wagon and followed the others down the trail toward the camp. Our only cargo, a mysterious chest shrouded in canvas. I was dying to know what was in that chest, but I dared not ask. The wind blew in our faces as we headed down the trail, and the smell of turpentine filled the air with its pungent odor. You could have found your way just by following your nose. The sun was setting as we arrived in camp.

I started to shiver when I saw two of Father's new Bainbridge associates standing at the company store, waiting for Father. The one person missing was Aldridge, and I prayed he wouldn't show up.

We went upwind of the still to make camp. Father arranged for me to sleep on the wagon a couple hundred steps from the fire. The wagon was empty, and the chest, still covered, sat near the fire. Father and his friends began to drink and celebrate. I had no idea why.

It was near one o'clock in the morning when I heard Aldridge's voice joining in the celebration. I grabbed my things and climbed under the wagon so I might make a quick escape if he approached. It was hot and the skeeters were bad, so I hung my netting from under the wagon and kept covered best I could. It was better to be sweaty than eaten alive.

With a large iron rod, they began to strike at the front of the chest until the lock gave way and the chest was thrown open. The men gasped and smiled, pleased at what they saw in the chest. I knew the only thing that could get that reaction from my father was gold and silver. The men sat down around the chest and divvied up its contents.

It must have been about four o'clock in the morning when I saw Aldridge stir, quietly walking away from the fire into the darkness. I abandoned the wagon and headed for the edge of the woods, a wise move; for a few minutes later, I heard Aldridge asking in a teasing voice, "Where are you girly? It's your old friend come to visit." Unable to find me, he cursed in quiet outrage.

"Shit, shit, shit, where you hid girl?" He soon gave up and headed back to the fire.

I left and found a lean-to nearer to where people were sleeping. Here I felt safe to close my eyes and get a couple hours sleep before dawn.

At sunup, I woke to a familiar face, Ponder, an old Negro I knew from early days. I knew him when he worked the Milton Plantation up above Marianna near the Chipola River. Ponder and his wife, Miss Millie, helped to raise me. "Hi yah, Ponder," I said, and he looked at me like he'd been shot.

"You knowed Old Ponder, young Miss?"

"Course I do. It's me, Pearl, from back on the Milton Plantation. Don't you know me Ponder?"

Ponder dropped to his knees and held out his arms just like the old days and gave me a big hug. He held me back and looked me up and down, and with a big smile on his face, he declared, "Miss Pearl how long has it been? You done gone and got yourself all grow'd up. You a fetching young lady now. Old Ponder didn't recognize you 'cause you all grow'd up."

"Where's Miss Millie, Ponder? Is she here too?" I asked.

"No, no, I don't reckon she is. Ya see, Miss Pearl, she pass away a couple year ago and leave Old Ponder alone. I's so heart broke at losing my Miss Millie that Mr. Milton felt I'd never get over her, so he sold me down river to this here turpentine camp, and I been here ever since."

Heartbroken myself at the news, I reached out and patted him on the cheek, telling him, "I'll help you miss her, so you don't have to do it alone."

Turns out that my father had arranged with a camp overseer to have the driver of the camp supply wagon drop me off in Apalachicola. Ponder was the Negro they trusted to make the trip.

Concerned, Ponder asked, "I ain't a leaving you in Apalachicola all by yourself is I?"

"I got lots and lots of good friends in Apalachicola, so you don't need be frettin' about me none," I assured him.

I loaded my things and climbed aboard the wagon, feeling very pleased to be setting at Ponder's side. That was until we passed my father's camp. He was off a good distance, and I made sure he saw me on the wagon. Thank God, Aldridge had his back to me and took no notice.

A short distance down the road, I became concerned when I saw a little black child sitting on the ground, bawling. The child's mother was tied to an iron ring attached to the whipping stump. An overseer, a brute of a man, called Elias reached down and ripped the dress from the woman's back, exposing her flesh. Walking a short distance to his horse, he pulled a Cat o' nine tails from his saddle and returned standing over the woman.

I asked Ponder what she'd done to receive a whippin'? Turns out her only crime was trying to make it over to the nearby lumber camp to visit her husband who had been sold away.

Having spent the first years of my life among plantation slaves, and knowing the slave marriage vow, "until death or distance do you part," I also knew it had very little meaning when it came to the love between a man and a woman. For generations, paths were worn down between plantations, and slaves never missed an opportunity to travel the paths to visit loved ones on neighboring plantations. She wasn't running away. She would have returned. This was an injustice I could not bear to watch.

Sensing what I was about to do, Ponder reached out to try and stop me, but I was quick, and before he could hold me back, I leaped from the wagon. In a blinding rage, I ran up behind Elias and threw myself over the woman just as the Cat o' nine tails fell. I screamed out as the whip tore through my clothes, cutting into the flesh on my back. I turned to Elias, begging him to stop.

What happened next was like a nightmare. Father reached down, grabbed me, carried me to the back of the wagon, and threw me like a sack of taters into the wagon. Ponder caught me just before I hit the seat back. Screaming and shaking his fist at Ponder, Father yelled, "Nigger, don't you stop till you throw her out of that wagon in Apalach, and don't you touch those lashes. I want her to suffer all the way. Maybe it'll teach her to keep the hell out da other people's business. Now get her the hell out da my sight."

In that moment, Father had to have known he had gone too far. I truly believe Elias had a revelation standing witness to Father's uncontrolled rage. With a transformed look on his face, Elias bent over and unstrapped the woman from the stump and helped her to stand. Ponder, Elias, the woman, and child all stood in silence, staring at my father, dumbfounded by his reaction. Now, very self-consciously restrained, he called out, "Hold on there nigger." With a sly smile on his face, he tried to recover from his show of cruelty by passing me a pouch of coins.

"Here; you might need a little spending money. I got to take care of a few things. You can stay with the old nigger woman you like. I be back in a couple of months for the season and pick you up." Standing back, he signaled Ponder to drive on.

Sometimes it's funny the way things work out. The whipping stump was one of those places where ravens always gathered whenever they saw people. They knew after a whippin' there'd be little bits of flesh on the ground, and that was the makings for an easy meal. Today was no different, and as father spoke his last words, the ravens noisily gathered in the trees. I could see the scared look on his face, so keeping my voice low so not to spook Ponder, I told him, "Looks like some of Momma's dead folk showin' up to keep an eye on you and me."

You'da thought he'd been struck by lightning. Ponder cracked the whip, and we were away. I never looked back.

Just out of sight of the camp, Ponder pulled the reins and cried out, "Whoa, whoa." As he reached for his knapsack, he told me, "Miss Pearl, I's needs you to bare your back for Old Ponder, so's I can put a little salve on them wounds. It make you feel better ridin' down this rough path and keep the poison out your blood."

I pulled what was left of my shirt up and exposed my back. "Now Miss Pearl, this gonna' sting a little, but purdy soon it quit stingin' and feel a whole lots better. You got to trust Old Ponder.

"I trust you Ponder; get on with it," I told him.

Chapter X

Purpose

 I know that for some, God reveals himself in quiet moments of contemplation and prayer. I also know that for some, like me, with hard headed ways, who have trouble seein' the obvious, he'd have to reveal my true purpose in midair after bein' whipped and flung into the back of a wagon.

 Oh, how God sometimes works in painful and mysterious ways. Was it just coincidence that after all these years, one of the most trusted men I had ever known, one that helped raise me, was now driving me to Apalachicola?

 When I considered how many people there must be in the world, a chance meeting with Ponder was an unlikely accident. The great powers Miss Charity and the Vicar spoke of were now playing out in my life. I had trouble explaining to Ponder that the tears welling up in my eyes were not because of pain or distress but of joy because I had discovered my purpose.

 Excited, I asked, "Ponder, how would you feel if I were to tell you that soon you and your children will be free?"

 With a surprised and confused look on his face, he responded. "I don't rightly know what it is to be free. I always wished it for my children, and I suppose I'd be pleased to try some of that freedom 'fore I die, but what you gettin' at Miss Pearl? How is I ever gonna be free?"

Feelings were welling up in me and bursting out all over. I let out a yell that just about scared old Ponder right out of his seat although the pain in my back kept me from rising to the occasion.

"Ponder, you just keep a drivin, and trust Little Pearl that things are about to change." And with that thought in mind, I started figuring things out. My first stop when I got back would be to the Vicar.

As the wagon rolled along, Ponder and I were soon sharing old stories and catching up on all the goings on since we last saw one another. It wasn't long before it was as though we had never been parted.

After selling that gold watch, I knew when I counted all the gold down in the chamber, I was likely to be one of the richest people around. I got to thinking of how many families that money could bring back together and free, and not only free, but I could give them enough money to get a good start on a new life.

We left the Apalachee Trail and pulled onto the St. Joseph road, heading east along the bay. I was joyous in having found my purpose and thrilled to be so close to home. I may have left in June, but I'd be celebrating the fourth of July back with my friends.

We rode into town, and people I knew waved and greeted me, welcoming me back. Ponder said it was kind of like being in a parade, havin' me in the wagon. We drove down to Water Street along the river where he was due to pick up the camp supplies at Grady's Mercantile.

I tried my best not to look down Commerce Street as we passed, but I did, and the sight of Blood's Tavern drew dark thoughts and images back into my mind. Just like on the morning I found Bella, I felt myself losing pieces of time. I fought back by concentrating on my new purpose, trying to keep from dwelling on the one thing I could not change. I succeeded in holding the darkness back, for now.

By the time Ponder loaded, it would be too late to return, so he would spend the night in town and begin his journey back early next morning. I told him no matter what, don't leave town without talking to me first, and I made him promise.

My back was aching. I could feel my heart throbbing in the wounds, but it wasn't just my back, I was hurting all over. I walked down the street bent over, holding the front of my shirt tight in my hands, stretching it over my back, so it wouldn't rub against the wounds. As I walked down Chestnut toward Broad Street, I could see the Vicar sitting on the porch of the vicarage.

He was elated to see me. Running out, he opened the gate in the picket fence. "Pearl," he yelled. He knew straightaway something was wrong and helped me onto the porch. Sitting on the swing, he asked me, "What's happened?"

But the questions weighing heavy on my mind were more important so I asked him a question first. "Vicar if someone was to come across some charms of some value, could this person use the charms to help her friends?"

"Yes, if they had value I suppose they could Pearl. I'd have to see one to tell you for certain. What is it you think you have?" the Vicar asked.

I started to relay the story of the slave woman at the turpentine camp and how I thought it was my purpose to free the Negroes so they could have their families back. When I told him about the whipping, he pulled my shirt up and looked at my back. The Vicar started to cry, which started me crying. Everything bad that had happened in my life came pouring out into my mind, and I began to fall apart.

The Vicar handed me his handkerchief, and I wiped my eyes, but I couldn't stop crying. Suddenly, like with Bella, I started seeing things in bits and pieces. Sometimes I was there, and sometimes I wasn't. I remember the Vicar carrying me down the street. I remember seeing Doc Chapman's face. The next thing I knew it was late afternoon. I was laying on a bed with the Vicar holding my hand, telling me I'd be alright. Shortly after, it was Dr. Chapman who assured the Vicar I'd be alright. He told the Vicar that he'd take good care of me until after the Wednesday night prayer study. The Vicar left for the church, and as soon as Doctor Chapman left the room, I grabbed a few matches from the night stand and snuck out, making my way down toward the Charity House.

I secured the lantern I'd left in the front room of the Charity House and carried it around to the side by the Water Oak tree. I could see things were just as I had left them. Moving the brush and boards I used to hide the hole, I lit the lantern and proceeded down into the chamber. Doctor Chapman did a good job binding my wounds, and I could tell that I would easily be able to complete my undertaking without too much pain.

I slipped one of the small gold bars into my trouser pocket but had to remove it to tighten the rope that held up my pants. Once my pants were secure, I slipped the bar back into my pocket and made my way back up to the surface. It was getting dark, so I doused the lantern before I broke ground level. Carefully covering my tracks, I headed down to the Trinity to wait for the Wednesday night prayer service to end.

It must have been one of the shortest services on record 'cause the Vicar was walking around the corner of the Trinity as I was walking up the path beside the church. I don't know who was more surprised to see me, the Vicar or Doctor Chapman who was walking down the street behind me. Doc Chapman never came all the way. He saw the Vicar, and as soon as he knew I was alright, he threw his hands up in the air, made some comment under his breath, and turned to walk home.

"Pearl, what are you doing? I told you I'd come to collect you after the service," he scolded.

Reaching in my pocket with both hands, I removed the gold bar. Struggling under the weight, I held it out, and placed it in his hands. The Vicar, falling to his knees asked, "Is this one of your charms?"

"This is just one of the small ones. I have lots and lots more where this one came from," I told him.

The Vicar started crying, but this time I saw a look on his face like the one I'd seen earlier on Elias's face. In that moment, the Vicar seemed transformed, as though a new life now lay before him. I could see the Vicar was overflowing with grace.

What I saw in his face reminded me of a picture I once saw where Jesus was standing outside a door with no latch. I figured the Vicar just opened his door from the inside and let Jesus in. I just knew that someday that would be the look on my face when I opened my door.

The Vicar said he needed time to think and told me we would talk in the morning. Excited, I told him, "Some things can't wait till morning." And I told him about Ponder and how it was important that he find him and keep him in town. "Ponder will be my first, and I need your help to free him," I said.

"I'll do everything in my power to do as you ask. Please let me take you over to Miss Caroline's for tonight. She'll be so happy to see you. Miss Pearl, if you'll allow me, tomorrow, I'll be happy to help you start making plans to free all your friends," and he gave me a most loving smile.

I, of course, held out my hand to shake on the deal, and it made the Vicar chuckle.

We walked hand in hand the two blocks over to the Florida Boarding House. I can't even describe the fuss Miss Caroline and the girls made over my return. Laying down on that feather bed, I felt I was home. My thoughts tonight wouldn't be of death and slavery, but of one very important task before me. I had to find Miss Caroline a husband.

Miss Caroline and Lottie were waiting outside my door when I woke, wanting to dress my wounds. Miss Caroline had already been over to Doctor Chapman's office for instructions. I felt it was bad enough that I showed up injured. The last thing I wanted was for Miss Caroline to think I attracted trouble, so I decided to tell her mostly just the good parts of my journey and very little of the bad.

After a most wonderful breakfast, I excused myself, anxious to visit the Vicar, but before I left, Miss Caroline made me promise to return for dinner at noon to catch up. I was so happy to see Miss Caroline and so grateful that she cared so much. I hugged her and never wanted to let go.

As I approached the Trinity, I was very pleased to see Ponder sitting on a bench under a Live Oak in the church yard. He was holding a piece of paper in his hand, and as I approached, he gazed at me with love and awe.

"Miss Pearl, I can't read, but the preacher he say this here paper say Ponder is free. Is it true, Miss Pearl? Does this little piece o' paper make me free?"

I was pleased to be able to tell him yes. Filled with joy, I told him we would start searching for his children, and they would soon be joining him. I assured him he would spend the rest of his life a free man.

"You need to be thinkin' 'bout where you want to live," I told him.

"I won't be goin' nowheres Miss Pearl. After the preacher give me this paper, I had a long talk with God, and he tell me my place is at your side helpin' any way I can. That is if you'll have me."

I wanted to hug him so badly, but people were watching, and he and I both knew that because he was black, for his sake, it was not a good idea.

The Vicar joined us at the bench, and we discussed the best way to proceed. Ponder listened, but not knowing what a charm was, limited his understanding. I assured him he would soon be in the thick of things because I'd need someone I trusted to help me move the charms. The Vicar would arrange for accommodation and monies needed for Ponder's room and board.

The Vicar suggested and Ponder agreed, that it was best if he'd be referred to as a slave from up on the Milton Plantation. If asked, we'd say that as a tithe, Mr. Milton bound him to the Trinity for some needed repairs. I told the Vicar, it's a good thing you can't go to hell for telling little lies that help people 'cause I got the feeling we was gonna have to be tellin' some whoppers. The Vicar agreed, but I could tell he was hesitant because he felt he was corrupting me. I assured him that was not the case.

The Vicar became my anchor. It was as though the same fire that burned in me now illuminated the Vicar. I knew we had both found our purpose in the same cause.

After our meeting at the Trinity, I took Ponder down to meet Miss Charity. I figured I could kill two birds with one stone by telling them at the same time. I would need them both if the plan was to work.

I was pleased to find Miss Charity in good health and high spirits. I introduced Ponder, and it was under the Magnolia tree beside Miss Charity's shack that I began to tell them my tale. It was as though a heavy burden lifted from me as I confided my deepest hopes and fears with two of the people I trusted most in the world.

Miss Charity clapped with joy and held out her arms to embrace me. "Child o' mine, I's so happy. God showed you your purpose. I knew you be special blessed by God his self."

Miss Charity and Ponder were like me. They couldn't care less about gold and riches but were excited about the freedom it would soon purchase.

As though ordained, everything fell into place in July 1859. The Ormans left to visit family in Syracuse, New York, just after the cotton season ended in June. Other than Miss Charity, most of the Orman's thirty-five slaves were upriver working at the Orman's Owl Creek Plantation, preparing the ground for citrus groves. Slaves who remained in town cared for Orman's Apalachicola properties, but it was Miss Charity who was in charge of the Orman House.

The timing and location were perfect. The Orman's house sat isolated on the bluff at the end of High Street. Unnoticed, Ponder, Miss Charity, and I could easily move some of the gold bars to a more accessible place for transfer to the Vicar, and I knew exactly where that place was. I led them into Miss Charity's shack, and we all stood dwarfed in front of my wardrobe. Our first job would be to make a few changes to this beautiful, enormous, box of freedom. Ponder took the lead. He had wonderful ideas on how we could make it work and still keep the gold secure.

It was close to noon when I left for the visit I promised Miss Caroline. Miss Charity and Ponder were unloading the wardrobe, getting it ready to store some of the gold. My back was starting to hurt, so I hurried, best I could, back toward Miss Caroline's. I just knew she'd insist on me staying with her, and the thought of being one of the girls again suited me fine. I was looking forward to getting back into one of my dresses.

In order to make an example of those who tried to run, Elias had tied iron nails into the ends of those nine cat tails. As I walked, my sweat was making the lashes burn and was slowing me down. I figured at the time this would be a good reminder to keep me focused on my purposes. I'd seen slaves take twenty and thirty lashes. I had but one lash on my back, and I felt no right to complain.

Miss Caroline was a regular mother hen when it came to taking care of me and was waiting with a tin of salve and clean dressings for my back. It was as though she knew and felt when I was in pain.

We ate at the small table on the front porch of the restaurant facing Centre Street. Lottie and Ava occasionally stopped by when they weren't serving customers. I knew I would have to be cautious. Miss Caroline was a master of getting me to talk, and if I wasn't careful, pretty soon she'd have me spilling all my secrets. I'd be embarrassed and ashamed for her to know all the terrible things I'd done. I believed in my mind, that if she knew, when the time came, she wouldn't want me. I felt no choice but to hold my tongue.

Lottie and Ava joined us after the noon rush, and the conversation became very lively when Miss Caroline's love life came up. She had evidently been approached by a suitor who took her down to the theater where they were entertained by a traveling troupe of players, but it sounded as though the show was much better than the suitor who she described as a combination of a choir director and her father.

I knew I had an ace up my sleeve, and I believed this to be the perfect time. I told them about meeting the prettiest man I had ever seen aboard the *River Bride*. I went on and on, telling them about his wonderful stories and how charming and handsome he was—all in the hope of peaking Miss Caroline's interests.

My mistake was in mentioning the name, Captain Hatch Wefing. The table erupted in laughter. Lottie immediately described him as a scurvy dog, just before Ava used the word womanizer. Miss Caroline evidently not only knew of Captain Hatch Wefing but had grown up under the power of his charm, and in her best stage voice, she dramatically stated, "Alack and alas, it was simply not to be, for my Captain had a wandering eye."

I was laughing so hard at all her drama I nearly wet myself. She explained how Captain Hatch was a beloved local philanderer, and over the years, because of his reputation, the local ladies learned to enjoy his company at arm's length. They told me not to feel bad about being taken in; he seemed to have a mysterious power over all the ladies. I didn't tell them it wasn't about me. My disappointment was in losing the only name on my list of suitors for Miss Caroline.

I changed the subject by telling them about how I met Odila and Zelig at the springs and how Odila and I had become close friends. I recited the letter I memorized word for word and told them I would have to go downtown and find a store that could sell me one of those new metal-dip pens, paper, and ink so I could compose my first letter.

I showed them that the money was not a problem, and they gasped when I held out a twenty-dollar gold piece. I don't know what they would have done if I'd held out all eighty.

Miss Caroline was very proud of me for wanting to write the letter. She put Lottie in charge of the boarding house and walked with me downtown. She said she knew the perfect place to purchase writing supplies. I spent an hour picking out my first metal-dip pen, and then I found out it came in its own shiny silver case, at no extra charge. It was by far the finest purchase I had ever made.

Miss Caroline set me up on the table in the parlor, and she, Lottie, and Ava all hovered around me helping to make the letter perfect. When it was finished, I carefully folded the letter and put it in the envelope. I addressed the envelope to Freud Mill Works Supply, and underneath that, I wrote "Miss Odila Freud." On a third line, I wrote "Bainbridge, Georgia."

The post office was down the street, so we all walked together. They watched as I requested a stamp from the postman.

The postman weighed my letter and said, "Two Ben Franklin's coming up," and handed me a stamp with a picture of the man that I believed must have been named after the steamboat. After a chuckle, the postman corrected my history and charged me ten cents for two, five cent stamps.

A five-cent stamp would carry a one-half ounce letter up to three hundred miles. I was rather proud that my letter, because of the paper quality and three pages, weighed almost an ounce.

He said he was out of Washington's—those were ten cents, and then I'd only need one stamp. A ten-cent, Washington stamp could send a one-half ounce letter over three hundred miles or could send a one-ounce letter under three hundred miles. I told him that's alright since it was the same price. I liked the color better, and two stamps would make the envelope look much more important.

I whispered to Miss Caroline, and she quietly told me that licking the back would make them sticky, and she pointed to the place they needed to be stuck. I asked the postman a lot of questions because I felt in the future I could become one of his better customers.

I slipped out early next morning and ran to the post office to check the mail for a response and was rather discouraged to see my letter in the same slot as the day before. At breakfast, I told them about my letter not being delivered. Miss Ava laughed so hard milk came out of her nose. Miss Caroline said she'd give me a lesson on patience being a virtue a little later in the day.

Chapter XI

Freedom Be Gold

    I found great meaning in my new purpose, and I put all my efforts into working hard and learning everything I could. If I wasn't helping at the Florida Boarding House, I'd help clean the Trinity. My most important job, that turned out to take the least amount of time, was moving gold. Once we got it all set up, it was easy. It amazed me how many slaves you could buy with just one of those big bars of gold. I figured soon enough, every one of them would be free.

    Taking a block and tackle from the Orman's mule barn, Ponder climbed up on the Charity House roof to tie it off high enough in the Water Oak tree so the bottom pulley didn't get in the dirt. Miss Charity sewed two, heavy canvas bags together, and we attached her bag to the end of a rope long enough to reach the bottom of the chamber. We tied the other end of the rope off to the tackle. We figured the bag would do nicely to hold a few bars of gold. We soon realized when it came to moving gold, the size of the bag had nothing to do with it; it was all about the weight of the gold.

    I'll never forget the look on Ponder's face the day he first set foot in the chamber and saw all the gold, and I'll really never forget the look on his face when he worked his way around the room and came across that pirate's skeleton gawking at him. I'd completely forgot about the pirate. Ponder nearly passed out. He was gasping for air and backing up the whole time. I threw a piece of sail cloth over my pirate friend, but by the time I turned back around, Ponder was gone. I caught up with him topside. Shaking and as pale as a sheet, he was talking so fast, he was hard to understand.

"Miss Pearl, I do most anything you ask me, but I ain't a workin' down dare with no dead people. I ain't a goin' down dar till he get buried proper, and dat's all they is to dat." He sat down on the ground, trying to catch his breath.

Just the mention of that pirate glarin' at him and he'd turn back pale. He found no humor in what just transpired and made it clear he didn't think too kindly of me and Miss Charity gigglin' and thinkin' otherwise.

We didn't get much gold moved on the first day. I went back down into the chamber and disassembled the pirate's bones. Loading them into the bag, Ponder hoisted them up. We dug a nice grave and held a funeral for the pirate. Miss Charity even read a few verses out of the Bible over his grave. After that, Ponder was fine about goin' in the hole.

The first problem we faced was Ponder couldn't be in two places at the same time. He needed to be in the chamber to load the gold bars into the bag, and he had to climb out to hoist the bag out of the hole. I finally told Ponder just to stay down there. I thought I could pull it up by myself.

Ponder seriously doubted I possessed the strength to raise the bag but finally relented, and in a sarcastic voice told me, "Go ahead and pull. You just give a holler when you want I should climb out this hole an pull dat rope."

Just as Ponder predicted, I was having trouble pulling the bag up. That's when I had one of my greatest ideas. I told Ponder to stay put. I tied a loop in the end of the rope, slung it over my shoulder and climbed the ladder onto the roof of the Charity House. Grabbing the rope in my hands, I stuck my foot in the loop and jumped.

It was a gentle drop to the ground. The bag came flying out of the hole, swung out, and fell on the ground spilling its cargo. I simply walked over, picked up the bag, and threw it back in the hole. Ponder was in awe. I know because even top side, I could hear him say, "How da hell she do dat?"

"Just funning around," I yelled down. "You got that bag loaded yet?" I could hear him chuckling.

Miss Charity was sitting in a chair, shelling pecans over by High Street, but what she was really doing was keeping watch. Good thing too, 'cause when she walked over and saw me jumpin' off that roof, she had a regular conniption fit. Yelling down into the hole, she asked, "Ponder, you put her up ta dis?"

Being down in the chamber, Ponder had no idea what was going on topside. Miss Charity insisted that I stop no matter how well my system worked. Me and Ponder didn't see it as bein' such a bad idea, so in the future, when Miss Charity was watchin', Ponder would run both ends of rope, but when she wasn't lookin', I was jumpin'.

The first bars we transferred in the Vicar's carriage down to the vicarage. The Vicar arranged to have an elder fill in a few Sundays while he traveled up-river to Tallahassee to get our plan up and running. He purchased small amounts of acreage in remote areas in four Northern Florida counties. These would be what he called our staging areas.

Slaves would be purchased and sent to one of these small holdings where they received their freedom papers and started the journey out of the south. The Vicar knew lots of people who felt as we did, and for a while, they willingly gave up their lives to help in my cause. The Vicar's right hand man was a free black named Matthew. Miss Charity glowed whenever she heard his name mentioned. Matthew was a minister and Charity's oldest son.

To make the gold more accessible, we hauled some of the bars, a few at a time, in a wheelbarrow up to the wardrobe. Ponder did a wonderful job preparing the wardrobe to hold the bars. Not only could we fill the hollow base, but he made it so the floorboard inside the base could be removed. Under the shack, he built a wooden box clear to the ground, and that box held an equal amount of gold.

After laboring a week, we finished. Down in the chamber, among all the stacks of gold bars, it was hard to tell that any gold had been removed, but our coffers were full. Ponder built a heavy, cypress door and mortared it into the stone wall of the chamber, and we carefully covered our tracks.

At the house, we stood looking into the wardrobe, ready to put the board back into the base when Miss Charity said it best. "If you could see freedom…, dat be its color. Freedom be gold."

***

Nearly five months passed, and well into November, our secrets still remained cloaked in shadow. I worried about the Vicar. He seemed to be aging at a rapid pace, but when I spoke to him, I knew it made no difference because to him, no matter the condition of his body, his spirit now burned with a white-hot flame. The Vicar had never been so alive.

Father had been gone a long while now, and my life was better for it. I know it was wrong, but I prayed he'd never return. I also found myself very distraught because after posting numerous letters to Odila, they'd yielded no response. I began to worry that I might have done something wrong. Maybe she was upset because I didn't see her before I left.

That started me thinking of the chest father and Aldridge loaded onto the wagon at Bainbridge. I just knew that chest was somewhere at the turpentine camp, and within the empty box I could find the answers I sought.

With so much accomplished since my return, why did I feel myself falling into despair?

***

Soon, it was December, and my despair faded as Christmas grew closer. The rains were late, and the river was low. I figured that was why father hadn't reared his ugly head. He was probably holed up somewhere waiting for the cotton shipping season to begin, and I didn't have a problem with that.

I was spending a lot of time learning how to decorate, and between the Trinity and the Florida Boarding House, my bow tying was much improving. Miss Caroline needed my help with the baking and candy making. I was her head taster although sometimes I had to fight Lottie over a frosting bowl.

It was an honor when the ladies of the church asked me to lay baby Jesus in his crib. I stood back and looked at him lying there in the straw and started crying for no good reason. I couldn't believe how I was quickly turning into such a crybaby girl.

I bought gifts for everyone, but my very best gift, I gave to Ponder. He was spending Christmas with two of his children whom we had found and purchased from an Alabama cotton plantation. After the holiday, they'd be moved to our land holding in Washington County for relocation to either a Free State or Canada.

The rain started falling December twenty-first, and it didn't stop till the twenty-fourth. The river was rising and would soon bring the cotton to fill our warehouses. It seemed as though nothing could dampen the spirit of the town, and Christmas went off without a hitch. It wasn't until Wednesday, December twenty-eighth the bottom fell out.

It was one o'clock Wednesday afternoon when I found myself walking down the street, wearing my new dress. Miss Caroline made the dress for me for Christmas. When I first asked to wear it outside, she told me flaunting was a form of vanity and a sin, and I should wait till Sunday. But a few minutes later, for unknown reasons, she changed her mind and said, on second thought, it might be best if I were to break it in.

She said if I walked down to the Post Office to check on the mail and then over to the Trinity to show the Vicar my new dress and came straight back, it wouldn't count as much of a sin.

It was a disappointing day for mail; our slot was empty, not that it mattered all that much. I was still looking forward to the Vicar's reaction when he saw my new dress. On the porch of the Post Office, as my shoe touched the first step, I heard a familiar but repressive voice, and my heart began to ache.

"Hey girl. Don't you look purdy. Don't be fearin'. I know we parted bad, but it's all behind us now. No hard feelin'. Come sit fer a minute, and let me tell you some good news fer a change."

I knew if I ran away, he'd find me and possibly hurt my friends, so I turned to face my father. He motioned for me to sit on the bench beside him, and I did.

Turns out, he hadn't been working cotton and turpentine at all. Instead, he'd just arrived back from New Orleans and was eager to tell me his good news. We'd soon be leaving for New Orleans where he and Aunt Etta would be wed.

"Won't it be nice havin' a momma Pearl? We gonna make a real nice family. Your cousins is lookin' forward to seein' you. Best be sayin' bye to your friends, 'cause we be leavin' in a week. You go ahead now and run along, and I'll catch up with you a little later."

I held my tongue but wanted so badly to scream out, "I'd rather die!" I hurried away to the Trinity.

My prayer was answered when in the church yard I saw the Vicar and Miss Charity sitting together on a bench under the live oak. It was my good fortune that the Vicar had been run out of the church for Miss Sadie's ladies meeting, and Miss Charity was there attending Miss Sadie.

I must have looked terrible because they didn't even notice the dress; they simply asked what was wrong.

"My father's back, and he's taking me to New Orleans," I told them.

Suddenly, they both turned pale as me. I explained what father had said. The Vicar, knowing my distress, assured me in no uncertain terms, he would sooner burn in hell than let that happen.

"But why, after all these months?" he asked.

"Ransom," said Miss Charity. "Her family want her back, and they is willin' to pay ta get her back. Them two scoundrels finally found a reason to keep her alive."

Chapter XII

Salt

"Pearl, I want you to go quietly and start packing. I'll be over directly to talk with Miss Caroline." Turning to Miss Charity, he told her, "Charity, take Sadie's carriage and find Ponder; tell him it's time. If Miss Sadie asks, I'll tell her I sent you over to pick up the church mail. Pearl, I'm sorry to be telling lies, but you need to trust me. Now more than ever, we need to keep our secrets. The fewer people that know, the safer we'll all be."

I hurried back to change my clothes and pack. I sat on the edge of my bed until I heard the Vicar knock. Cracking the door, I listened as he explained that Father had returned and wanted to steal me away and how instead, he had arranged for me to stay with friends somewhere safe. Miss Caroline readily agreed but didn't like that he would not reveal the location.

Miss Caroline and I both began tearing up as I approached with my bags in hand. The Vicar asked for pen and paper and schooled me in writing a note saying I was running away. He planned to show the note to my father, so he would leave Miss Caroline and my friends alone.

The Vicar went for a stroll and located Father in a pub. Quickly returning, we slipped unseen out through the back door. Ponder was waiting in the Vicars carriage two blocks away on Columbus Street.

Ponder needed no instruction. The Vicar simply helped me into the carriage, and Ponder cracked the whip. That's when I realized this had all been rehearsed, and I was just along for the ride. We headed west along the bay onto the St. Joseph Road.

It was late evening when we arrived at the salt works on Cape San Blas. Without salt as a preservative, the south could not exist, hence being worth one's weight in salt was a high praise. Armed men guarded the entrance, but they immediately stepped aside when they saw the Vicar's carriage approaching. The workers were gathered around a fire in the communal area in the center of the camp.

They gazed silently as the carriage came to a halt. I looked to Ponder, but like me, he knew none of these people. They crowded around, helping us down from the carriage. I could not comprehend why the ladies in the crowd were gently reaching out and touching me. The crowd parted as a large Negro man approached.

Ponder tensed and gripped his fists, but I held him back. I saw no evil in this man's eyes. There was something familiar in his face, but I was at a loss to distinguish it. He picked me up, hugged me tightly, and carried me over to the fire. Ponder, confused, was being patted on the back and prompted to follow.

Looking upon their faces, I noticed a great diversity in this gathering. Black slaves, Irish, Italian, Greek, and others I did not recognize stood together, crowded around this communal fire.

My father commanded through fear and intimidation, but I knew if his only means of gaining power was by thrashing another man into submission, it didn't make him right. Men like Ira Sanborn commanded through money. Achieving power by these methods was fleeting at best. Too many men inherited their power and then abused it, never having learned the disciplines required to earn it for themselves, but this black man was different. I saw it in the faces of the crowd as they looked upon him. I heard the respect and admiration in the silence of the crowd as he approached; he was commanding power through his mere presence.

"You're Ponder, and you are our Pearl," the black man said with a sincere smile.

"Yes, I'm Pearl," I responded.

"Welcome to your camp, Apalachicola Pearl. I am Matthew."

Surprised, I stated, "You're one of Miss Charity's babies. You're a lot bigger than I figured."

Everyone laughed seeming to find humor in what I said. Feeling more at ease, they talked among themselves. Ponder and I sat talking with Matthew well into the night.

In my short life, I'd stood witness to some of the greatest orators of our day. Long orations were common for the times. For a fee, these men of many words would come and speak at one's church or organization. They would expound for hours on the sins and virtues of modern thinking and on the understanding of general issues of the day.

You might have to pay for an orator, but chances were, you'd learn something of value. Politicians spoke for free but rarely had anything of value to say. Looking back, I'd have to say politicians were a lot more fun, and rotten vegetables didn't have to go to waste. Matthew, on the other hand, spoke with the heart of a poet and was the finest orator I had ever heard.

I understood why the Vicar chose Matthew. As a freed slave, he was wise in the ways of plantation life, and being a minister gave him access to many camps and plantations where he was allowed to minister to slaves.

It was Matthew who taught me the harsh realities of slavery and how hard it was to drive generations of bondage out of a black slave.

For many of those we helped, freedom was a concept they could not easily conceive, and the South, good or bad, was the only home they knew. Places like the Salt Works allowed them time to adjust, and when their minds became free, they were better suited to choose their own path. In the meantime, while they learned how to be free, they were paid a fair wage and took great pride in helping to further the cause of freedom for others.

The Salt Works was very profitable, producing two to three hundred bushels of salt a day. The profit went to the owner and master, one Horace Rutledge, my very own Vicar. Under new ownership, the overseers and those hostile to the cause were dismissed, and those sympathetic to the cause were brought in to replace them. For those held as slaves, I wished I could have been there to see the looks on their faces when Matthew and the Vicar stood side by side and announced, "You are now free."

With the profits, the salt works not only supported itself but appeared aboveboard to the newly formed Confederate government. This camp added to the coffers that supported our cause. It was ironic that although the salt supported our confederate boys, the money from its sale supported Yankee causes.

The camp was a city unto itself with men whose sole job was to fish and hunt, supplying meat for the butcher and smoke house. Some were skilled in tanning and leather work. There was even a blacksmith's shop for the welding and repair of iron. Our mercantile was well supplied by the incoming steamers who bartered trading goods for salt. Back in the old country, one Irishman's wife was a teacher, and she started a school for the children. All things considered, the camp was a tolerable place to hide out.

At times, I found myself saddened by the fact that my cause and this camp were necessary at all. I couldn't help but believe that most men knew there was something fundamentally wrong with slavery. But wealth and power are blinding, and cheap labor meant high profits, often robbing a man of his good virtues. The devil was skilled in leading men to believe that after the fortune was made, there would be time to make amends for the roll they played in slavery. The sad truth was there were many masters who considered a slave nothing more than livestock and would never feel the need to seek forgiveness.

The forgiveness men would eventually seek would have to encompass more than just profiting on the backs of their own slaves but instead for all the slaves that suffered and died along the way. I could see the carnage of slavery ran deep in my country. The Vicar used my concerns about slavery to hold my interest when helping me to read and write. He once had me read a declaration then spent the entire afternoon helping me understand the words.

"All servants imported and brought into the Country… who were not Christians in their native Country… shall be accounted and be slaves. All Negro,

mulatto and Indian slaves within this dominion… shall be held to be real estate. If any slave resists his master… correcting such slave, and shall happen to be killed in such correction… the master shall be free of all punishment… as if such accident never happened."
—Virginia General Assembly declaration, 1705.

It became clear to me that slavery had plagued my country from the beginning. Sometimes at night I would lay awake imagining a slave master standing before the throne of God sighting the feeble laws of man as justification for slavery and for breaking his commandment "You shall not murder."

It wasn't fair, I was too young to have been burdened with the realization that my country was founded on the extermination of one race and the enslavement of another.

Black slave labor fueled the economy of the Southern plantations, lining the pockets of the aristocracy. But when it comes to cheap labor, Commerce doesn't care about the color of skin; to be a poor white immigrant was one small step above being black. Indentured servitude was illegal on both ends of the trade, but contracts were still signed. Calling it indentured servitude or simply a debt to a company store, made no difference in the final tally, it was still slavery. Turpentine and lumber camps were filled with immigrants, like the Irish, enslaved by these contracts.

I was pleased to find that the freedom we offered was extended to those whites held in indentured contract or enslaved by debt. According to Matthew, God only looked at souls of people, and in his eyes, we all looked the same. It was through the eyes of commerce that slavery knew no color.

Freeing the white indentures gave us an army of white faces who gladly escorted our freed black slaves to the north. Matthew was the perfect general for our army. He knew the plantations and work camps. He knew who could be trusted and those who were worthy of freedom. I had had no idea that the Salt Works was one of our staging areas.

All I did was place a single bar of gold in the hands of the Vicar, and crying, tell him what must be done. I could not comprehend how my little ripple of freedom had grown into this mighty wave of reform. Throughout the panhandle, hundreds of people of good conscience toiled, having pledged their allegiance to my cause.

Ponder, worrying that we might have been seen leaving town, spent the night with a club in his hand, sitting on a stool in front of my shack. Next morning, I gave him a hug and thanked him. Matthew came over and told Ponder to get some sleep, assuring him there was not a man in camp who wouldn't give his life in my defense. Words I found upsetting. I could not bear the thought of someone dying on my account.

The camp's towboats pushed the barges of salt out to waiting steamers for transport to market and returned with supplies and news on a regular basis. Matthew made sure someone would keep me updated on my father's whereabouts and the well-being of my adopted family in Apalachicola. The bad news was that it was approaching June, the end of the cotton season, and my father was still searching for me.

Chapter XIII

Rebel Guard

I was heartbroken knowing he did not search out of love. The deal he and Etta made with the family for my return must have been substantial.

My new friends at the camp warned Ponder and I that father was bringing together a group of ruffians into what he called his "Rebel Guard." The threat of a terrible war was coming to fruition, and he believed a gang of land pirates might find great rewards in the carnage soon to follow.

The Vicar's ploy with my runaway letter had worked. When Father confronted him, he handed him the letter, and Father found no reason to question any further. To date, I don't believe Miss Caroline or Miss Charity could have picked my father out of a crowd. They were lucky.

As soon as I found myself alone, in a spiteful voice, I screamed out, "Damn his eyes." With the creation of the Rebel Guard, Father's search would widen far beyond Apalachicola. I would have to remain at the Salt Works waiting for the end of the cotton season, praying his money would run out, and he might move on. Now more than ever, I needed to be cautious.

The Salt Works was in need of a new, shallow-draft barge to transport salt to the steamers offshore. The boat works on the river north of Apalachicola was tasked with the job of construction, and we received word that the barge was complete and ready for pickup. The towboat *Fry*, would be dispatched to retrieve the barge and bring it back through the bay, out West Pass, and over to the Salt Works.

Knowing the proximity of the boat works to the turpentine camp got me thinking, and I soon found myself obsessing about finding the mysterious chest from Bainbridge. I just knew father and his cronies would have discarded the chest. I spoke with the salt-works foreman, Boss Clay, and explained my request. As it turned out, he was in need of two barrels of rosin to seal the old barges. It was a part of his plan to stop by the turpentine camp to pick them up. On such a small order, they could avoid a trip to the Narrows and simply float the barrels on a small boat down the Brothers River to the Apalachicola River.

I knew, for my own safety, I would not be allowed to leave the camp so my next stop was to visit Ponder. He was the one man who knew the turpentine camp better than me and stood a good chance of finding the chest. Papers were forged to identify him as a slave belonging to the salt works to keep him safe in his journey. Ponder accepted my request without hesitation.

I waved goodbye as the *Fry* pulled away. Ponder, with a determined look on his face, waved back. Ponder was a most faithful friend, and I began feeling regret, having asked him to go in the first place. I would spend sleepless nights until his safe return.

Allowing additional stops for supplies and rosin, the trip was scheduled to take five days, but it had already been seven. Mid-morning on the eighth day, I received word that one of the crew from the *Fry* just rode in on a mule with bad news. My heart sank, and I just knew something bad had happened to Ponder. I ran down to the camp office and barged in. Out of breath I tried to ask, but Boss Clay stopped me in mid-sentence and said, "Ponders fine. Sit a minute and catch your breath."

Sitting on the bench I listened as the men talked. It turns out that on the morning they were due to leave, the crew stoked the fire box under the boiler but didn't realize the water leaked out during the night and the fire burned the bottom of the boiler out. The *Fry* was now stranded at the boat works until a new boiler could be brought down from the Columbus Iron Works, and it would take about a month for the repair.

Boss Clay knew I was worried so when he finished with the crewman, he ordered him to sit with me on the bench and answer my questions. It was best this way, and Boss Clay knew not to put me off because without answers, I'd have pestered him until I was satisfied.

Jasper, the crewman, was very kind and explained how the *Fry* plied its way up the Apalachicola to the Brothers River. Here they launched a small skiff, and he and Ponder were tasked with retrieving the rosin barrels from the turpentine camp. Once loaded, they would float the skiff with the barrels back down to the Apalachicola River and rejoin the *Fry* at the boat works.

He and Ponder rowed the skiff through the pine forest to the turpentine camp road then caught a ride on one of the camp wagons to the still. They made the deal for the rosin, and while Jasper and the camp slaves hauled the barrels by wagon back to the skiff, Ponder stayed behind and began searching. After a day, Ponder became very discouraged when he was unable to find the chest.

Next morning they returned to the *Fry* to find that the boiler had been damaged when it was re-fired with no water. "When Ponder discovered it would be a month for repair he seemed pleased and was determined to return to the camp to search for your chest." Jasper relayed. "He knew how important it was to you and didn't want to let you down, so he headed back to the camp." I thanked Jasper for his kindness and we parted ways.

The overwhelming guilt I felt for sending Ponder into harm's way was unbearable. The last eight days were bad enough. I hated to think about a month of sleepless nights. I asked Boss Clay to tell anyone traveling in the area to find Ponder and send him home. I cried when on June twentieth, 1859, the *Fry* returned without Ponder.

***

Early Sunday morning, June twenty-sixth, found me sitting on the porch of my shack, missing my friend. The sun was just lighting the morning sky when through the mist, I saw Ponder walking up the camp road. I didn't mean to wake everyone, but I screamed his name in celebration and went running to greet him. I embraced my friend and scolded him at the same time for not returning with Jasper.

"I found dat chest Miss Pearl. Old Ponder found it." He boasted, struttin' like a rooster.

"Oh Ponder, if anything happened to you, I couldn't live with myself," I told him. It was as though an enormous weight lifted from my shoulders. I was so happy to see him return safe.

Returning to the porch, Ponder told me of the chest. He said he had nearly given up hope when he noticed a chest matching my description under the seat of one of the camp wagons.

The drayman found the chest discarded in the woods and was using it to hold the tools used to box cut the pines. Ponder described the chest to me in detail but said the drayman claimed he found the box empty. Upon closer examination, Ponder noticed a small brass plate nailed to the front corner of the chest, and when no one was looking, he pried it off and hid it in his pocket.

Proceeding over to where my father had camped months ago, and very close to the place where the drayman claims to have found the chest, Ponder searched the woodland for any signs that might point to the exact location. He soon came across the remnants of some papers, but they were badly weathered, having long since lost their print. He described them as falling apart in his hands when he attempted to pick them up.

He said he kept looking and not far away, hidden in the undergrowth, he spotted what looked like an oil skin pouch. It was covered in poison ivy, but that didn't stop him. He retrieved the pouch and added it to his pocket. This also explained the rash he was trying to hide with an old rag that he had wrapped around his right hand and wrist.

Ponder proudly pulled the pouch from his pocket and placed it in my hands. Unable to read, he was as anxious as a schoolboy for me to reveal the contents of the pouch. When I told him, "Not now," he complained all the way to the camp infirmary where I got an herb poultice made up to dry out that ivy rash.

Once back on the porch, I opened the pouch and removed the brass plate. My heart skipped a beat when I saw the initials F.M.W.S. engraved into the metal. I had long suspicioned that the chest belonged to the Freud Mill Work Supply.

Ponder looked over my shoulder as I read the documents from the pouch. They were copies of the receipts given to Ira Sanborn, showing payment in full for the machines my father and his cronies had delivered to the Sanborn's Estahatchee Mill. It was a substantial amount of money.

Hiding at the Salt Works gave me plenty of time to think. The camp teacher told me the best places to find information were at a library or a local newspaper. I knew my next stop would be a visit to the *Apalachicola Commercial Advertiser*. I needed to know the facts of what had happened on the day we left Bainbridge, Georgia.

It was obvious to me that father had stolen that money from Mr. Freud. Proving it would take more than an oil skin pouch with a few receipts some Negro found in the woods.

It was a substantial amount of money, but split four ways and knowing my father's habits, it wouldn't last very long. It was October before he finally left town. It was strange though; he left the mules and dray at the stable with the agreement they could rent them out and keep the money to cover the cost of feed. When father was last seen, he was heading up-river with his allies.

Arriving back in town, I immediately took notice of all the people. It was much busier than usual for this time of year. The summer heat had been tolerable, and with no signs of the yellow fever, many locals stayed in town, and some transients came back early.

I was very anxious to see Miss Caroline, Miss Charity, and the Vicar, but because of my obsession with that chest, instead of running straight to them, I found myself walking through the doors of the *Apalachicola Commercial Advertiser*.

A man with ink-stained fingers approached and inquired how he might be of service. I told him what I was looking for and the approximate date. He led me into the backroom and to a shelf containing stacks and stacks of papers. He selected one stack and placed it on a table in front of me.

"If your dates are correct, you should find what you're looking for somewhere in here. If I can be of any more assistance, please let me know. I'll be out front." He turned and proceeded back out to the press and began setting type.

It wasn't long before I was quickly scanning through the pages, looking for any article referring to Bainbridge, Georgia. I was there for about an hour when an article caught my eye. "Bainbridge, Georgia, Turpentine Still Explodes Killing Five." My hand began shaking as I read the words.

My heart was breaking as I read that Mr. Frederick Freud and three camp workers died in that explosion. It appeared as though the workers were attempting to free Mr. Freud after discovering him chained to the structure. It was thought the fire was started to distract the town and cover the tracks of a murderer. Freud Mill Work Supply had been broken into, but it was unknown if anything was missing. Mrs. Ida Freud was later discovered in her home, raped and with her throat slit. The town was now searching for the missing children: Odila, age seven, and Zelig, age four.

I couldn't believe what I was reading. The thoughts and rage running through my mind frightened me of myself. Miss Caroline read the paper, and I knew she had to have known. I'd sent a letter to Odila just before the article appeared in the paper. Why didn't Miss Caroline tell me?

Confused, I left to find the Vicar for counsel. I could not believe what Miss Caroline had done. I found the Vicar sitting and rehearsing his Sunday sermon in the front pew of the Trinity. He was happy to see me and I him, but he could tell by my face something was terribly wrong. "What's wrong child?"

I told him about the article and that Odila and Zelig were missing and about the terrible thing Miss Caroline had done by hiding it from me.

He stopped me in mid-sentence and scolded me for ever having thought badly of Miss Caroline. He asked if I remembered what happened the day Bella died.

"When you woke that afternoon, you thought it was the same day. Pearl, you were lifeless, laying in that bed for two days, and during that time, Miss Caroline never left your side. She loves you more than you can imagine, and she truly believed the news of your friend Odila might take you away from her forever. She wasn't willing to risk telling you until you were stronger or until she knew for certain about your friend."

How could I have ever thought badly of Miss Caroline? In tears, I hugged the Vicar and ran as fast as I could all the way to the Florida Boarding House, yelling her name, all the way. Miss Caroline couldn't help but hear me coming. I ran up the steps into her waiting arms. She was so pleased, but she had no idea why I was apologizing. I told her I read what the paper said of Odila and Zelig, and suddenly her concern was for my well-being. I assured her that although I was very sad, I would be all right. It was a grand reunion, and soon Lottie and Ava joined in.

Being young and having nothing to compare, I figured perhaps my life was really no different than anyone else's, but it did seem to me that, unlike most folks, death and evil followed in my wake. *What was I becoming?* The news that Odila and Zelig were missing didn't surprise me all that much. *Have I become so calloused that I no longer feel compassion?*

When I read the article from Bainbridge, it was as though I was someone else who didn't know the people involved. I questioned how I could feel so detached from such horrific news concerning my best friend.

For the sake of the cause, and the safety of my friends in Apalachicola, I felt it best to keep the sorted details of my life hidden away. For now, until my plan was complete, I put up a facade and tried to become more how I imagined myself, revealing less of my reality.

***

Christmas of 1859 came and went and was joyous enough, but a shadow cloaked our Southern lands. Our leaders spoke of a great army approaching from the north, slowly descending upon us with its hordes of Hessian mercenaries.

It made no sense to me that these men were my enemies. I didn't understand secession and felt that only a fool would die in the name of commerce over cotton, but I certainly understood the words that endeared me to my country and gave me purpose.

> "We hold these truths to be self-evident, that all men are created equal, that they are endowed by their Creator with certain unalienable Rights, that among these are Life, Liberty, and the pursuit of Happiness."

To my concerns, if Mr. Jefferson didn't want to include Negroes, he wouldn't have said all men. When it came to my cause, freeing the slaves, it seemed that the Yankees and I were in agreement. I would hold my judgment on these Yankees until I looked them in the eye and heard what they had to say.

***

It was mid-January 1860 before my father caught up with me. He enlisted the help of a passing U.S. Marshal to track me down. I had little use for U.S. Marshals. They stood in stark contrast to what I believed.

Since the Fugitive Slave Act of 1850, U.S. Marshals were nothing more than bounty hunters used to enforce the act. The abolitionists would refer to the act by a different name. They called it the "Bloodhound Laws." Corrupted by the lust for gold, their services were put on the block and sold to the highest bidder. Great profits could be found in the capture and return of escaped slaves from free Northern states. The bounties were high, and it didn't really matter if the Negro was slave or free, the money was still paid.

After making inquiries, the Marshal knew of my close ties with the Vicar, Horace Rutledge. A friend of mine, one of the local boys, stopped by and excitedly told me that a U.S. Marshal was down at the church asking questions about me. I handed him some coins and told him to keep his mouth shut and not to tell a living soul.

From what I could tell, Father and the Marshal had set up camp at the Trinity and, for the most part, were holding the Vicar hostage. I hated my father and despised him for what he was doing to the Vicar, but the hate I felt for my father was equaled by the love I felt for the Vicar. Father knew I would never let anything happen to the Vicar.

Father greeted me as I walked through the door of the vicarage with a self-righteous smile and his usual contempt. I could tell right away the U.S. Marshal was uncomfortable with the whole affair. Father extended his hand to the Marshal trying to release him from service, whispering to him, "We're square; you can go."

To the Marshal's credit, unintimidated, he stared back at my father and told him, "I think I'll stick around." In just those few words, I knew beyond a doubt, I was sold out for no more than a gambling debt. I could tell father was irritated by the Marshal's determination to stay.

I sat by the Vicar, holding his hand as father expounded on how much he'd missed me and his concerns for my well-being. He talked of how he and Etta put off the wedding, waiting for my return, so we could become a family together.

He claimed that in the meantime, having secured a good job, I would be able to stay with my friends. We wouldn't be returning to New Orleans until the fall, and maybe by that time, the Northern hostilities would end, and it would be safer to travel.

All I could do was glare at him. I'd had more than my fill of his sanctimonious ramblings and felt as though, at any moment, I might cry out in rage when suddenly, unexpectedly, he stooped down and took me by the shoulders, and after a kiss on my cheek, he whispered, "Girl, you foul my plans again, and I'll skin your Vicar and burn him alive." As he and the Marshal left, he told me, "I'll be checkin' in on you once in a while to make sure you're good."

Cold and unemotional, I responded, "Yes, Dray." I could tell it bothered him that I no longer acknowledged him as Father. I would never again allow him to hear the word Father pass my lips.

> Ephesians 6:4 "And, ye fathers, provoke not your children to wrath: but bring them up in nurture and admonition of the Lord."

> Colossians 3:21 "Fathers, provoke not your children to anger, lest they be discouraged."

I knew my scripture, and Dray was no father. He barely qualified as human. He had made the mistake of threatening my friends for the last time, and because of this, he was dead to me. All I had to do now was find a way to make it so.

After our encounter, I don't know who was shaking more, me or the Vicar. The Vicar was ready to hide me away, but I was insistent on staying in town. He asked me what my father had whispered. Not wanting to worry him, I told him those words remain between me and Dray. I made the Vicar promise not to say a word of this to anyone, especially not to Miss Caroline or Ponder. He reluctantly agreed, and I left heading back to Miss Caroline's.

Over the course of the next few months, I saw my father off and on, mostly down in the bowery at one of the taverns. He would leave for weeks at a time and travel somewhere up-river, sometimes alone and other times with one of his associates. Absent from the picture was that filthy bastard, Aldridge; I couldn't help but to wish him dead.

***

By the first week of February 1861, seven states had seceded from the Union, Florida being the third. On February sixth, the first Confederate Congress was held in Montgomery, Alabama, and on the ninth, Jefferson Davis was elected the first president of the newly formed Confederate States of America.

With no formal declaration, I still held out hope the war might be averted. February and March found the preparations for war well underway. The one thing missing was a Union presence. Even with no declaration of war, it appeared that just the threat had been enough to have an adverse effect on the cotton shipping season.

Chapter XIV

Prospecting

The last week of March of 1861 found Miss Caroline, Lottie, Ava, and I sitting on the porch of the boarding house, enjoying a nice breakfast and trying to talk about anything but the upcoming war when suddenly, Lottie and Ava started giggling and pointing. I looked over to Miss Caroline and watched as her face turned red as a beet.

They were pointing to a very tall man walking down Columbus Street. On the surface, I couldn't understand all the fuss. He was freakishly tall, well over six feet, and it was plain to see by his gait that he was gimpy in one leg. I had seen the man before, and it became immediately obvious Miss Caroline had taken notice of him too.

"You girls are incorrigible; he's an important man who doesn't even know I exist and moreover, wouldn't care less if I did," said Miss Caroline.

"Who is he?" I asked.

"Why that is Mr. Michael Brandon Kohler," said Ava in a witty, little voice.

"Girls, you stop it right now," said Miss Caroline, pointing her finger at them.

"All Ava's saying is that right now, the only figures he notices are in a ledger down at the Customs House. If he ever took notice of Miss Caroline's figure, he'd change his profession fast," Lottie proclaimed.

"Girls, I told you to stop it," scolded Miss Caroline.

"She's right. We should quit teasing," said Ava.

"Thank you," Miss Caroline said decisively, and she began rocking in her chair, but a moment later, she smiled and added, "If I could just get him to take his meal at the restaurant, I'll bet I could put some meat on those bones. I think he might take notice of my figure if he wasn't starving to death."

We all laughed, and Miss Caroline once again turned bright red.

I saw the way Miss Caroline's face lit up as Mr. Kohler walked by. What I needed to do was find a way to pull his head out of those ledgers and get him to look into Miss Caroline's eyes. All he really needed was a push in the right direction. I was sure that with my help, he would find it to be the best decision he ever made. I was anxious to meet Miss Caroline's future husband and size up my potential new father.

Tall and slender, Michael Brandon Kohler, was an imposing figure at six foot five. He wasn't nearly as pretty as Captain Wefing and was by no means the handsome, strapping figure I'd have imagined as a suiter for Miss Caroline, but facts would bear out that if Miss Caroline, being a good judge of character, saw potential, I now felt it my duty to vet and approve him. For the next few days, I'd have my work cut out for me, following him around.

It wasn't long before I became very impressed with Mr. Michael Brandon Kohler. He held the respected position of Customs Cutter for the Port of Apalachicola. Of all the government offices at the Customs House, his was by far the biggest and best. He was the proud owner of not one, but two, well-kept houses. They sat side by side looking onto Columbus Street just a short distance from Florida Boarding House, important so Miss Caroline would not have to walk so far to work.

He was very cordial and was often stopped for conversations in the street. His church going was slightly lacking, but he never used vulgar language and was always very kind and polite.

On one occasion, I witnessed him rescuing a foul-tempered snapping turtle from the street. Even after receiving a bite for his trouble, he resisted the temptation to throw the turtle. Instead, he gently put the turtle down before nursing his bloodied finger. I'm not sure, but he may have said a swear word under his breath, but it was so discrete, I didn't feel I should count that against him.

What really put the icing on the cake for me was when I found out his two best friends were Constable Jacob Foley and the one and only, Captain Hatch Wefing.

I truly believed I must have had a flaw in my character because even knowing what a philanderer Captain Hatch was, it didn't stop me from giggling whenever he smiled and tipped his cap. Although Jacob and Hatch were not suitable candidates for matrimony, I felt they would make for perfect uncles.

I was standing under the dock behind the Customs House, listening as Mr. Kohler attempted to convince Jacob that the upcoming war was not all cut and dried. Mr. Kohler didn't buy into all the political rhetoric, and he suspected the real reasons for the war were masked by a lot of patriotic fervor. Mr. Kohler was fighting a losing battle. Jacob was resolved to serve the Confederacy and enlist if his new country should ask.

Jacob Foley knew that some of Mr. Kohler's objections were based on his inability to serve because of his bad leg. Jacob told him that if it weren't for Old Hickory trying to eat him all those years ago, he knew that he'd sign up just to keep track of his friends.

Knowing there would be no resolution, Jacob changed the subject by pointing to a dock just up-river. "You remember the day Michael? You were lucky that Hickory only wanted your stringer of fish, or you'd be a goner," remarked Jacob.

"What I remember is you running up and pulling me back, putting yourself in harm's way. That's what I remember, the same kind of crazy stunt that someday will get you killed." With that said, Mr. Kohler hesitated; sighing and shaking his head, he embraced Jacob, letting him off the hook. By this time, I was holding back my tears.

Men were masters at hiding their feelings. I never knew a friendship between two men could ever be so strong.

Mr. Kohler and I just gained a strong connection through a mutual friend—Old Hickory. After they left, I sat wondering if Hickory could be a part of a larger unseen plan. I looked out over the river, and although I didn't see him, I had the feeling that somewhere in the tall grass, he was watching over me.

After several days, I discovered no obvious reasons why Mr. Kohler would not make an excellent suitor for Miss Caroline. I found my opening for a proper introduction on the evening of April tenth. I spotted Mr. Kohler sitting on a bench across from the Bowery, watching the pubs open for the evening trade.

It took a little lie to get me there. Good thing for me that Miss Caroline and Miss Charity didn't really know each other, except by reputation. I told Miss Caroline I'd be spending the night at Miss Charity's 'cause she was feeling poorly. It was just a small white lie, for a good cause.

I was wearing my best dress from Miss Sadie and placed a drop of vanilla extract behind each ear. I heard men were more attentive to women that smelled like food, and I really needed Mr. Kohler to pay attention.

I boldly walked up, stood at the tips of his boots, and curtsied. He was deep in thought and at first didn't even notice me.

"Evening, Mr. Brandon. How are you this evening?" I asked.

Smiling, he responded, "Hello. Fine. Thanks."

From here on, I took over the conversation discussing many topics of local interest and telling him a little bit about myself and my life here in town. It was just in passing I mentioned Miss Caroline and her interests in his well-being.

"You know, sometimes I go down to the Florida House and visit with Miss Caroline. She is very kind, and sometimes when my papa doesn't come home, she lets me eat with her boarders there at the Florida House Restaurant."

"She's a real good cook. Sometimes, when I visit her, we sit in the morning and have a tea or some breakfast, and we see you walk'n by on your way to work. 'There goes that nice-looking Mr. Brandon.' Miss Caroline always tells me. 'He should take his meals here at the restaurant. I'll bet I could put some meat on the bones,' she says."

I noticed him looking at his arm and realizing Miss Caroline was right. I continued because I knew how important it was that he know Miss Caroline was unattached.

"She's a nice lady. She said she lost her husband three years ago. I never seen her lookin' for him, so he must be lost good 'cause I think Miss Caroline has given up find'n him. Do you know Miss Caroline?" He nodded his head yes.

"But not very well," he responded.

"You'd like her a lot. She's pretty and a real good cook," I told him.

"I'd heard she was a good cook," he said smiling.

I could tell by the gleam in his eye I had peaked his interest, but not wanting to overplay my hand, I quickly changed the subject. After a few more minutes of general conversation, I curtsied and bid him good night. Now I just needed to keep an eye on him for a couple of days to see if my little seed of matrimony would take root. If not, knowing how simple-minded men could be, I might have to plant a few more seeds.

I watched Mr. Kohler rise and head toward home, having made a wise decision not to visit the pubs. I took his place on the bench and was feeling very good about how well things had gone when I saw Miss Dixie Belle approaching from across the street.

Along with the Customs House, Court House, and Post Office, Miss Dixie Belle was considered a local institution. She was called by many, "A woman of questionable reputation." One of the lyrics of that new song that went, "Away, away, away down south in Dixie," took on a whole new meaning in Apalachicola. I had known her most of my life and liked her immensely.

Her memory was like mine. She could recall past events down to the last detail. Growing old, she had lost some of her looks, but she could still make a good living just talking about the old times and reminding the old men of how they were once young and virile. She was in the business of making men feel good about themselves, and no one was better at it than Dixie Belle.

"Why, Pearl, I do declare if you ain't the definition of purdy, then I don't know what purdy is. How you been girl?"

"Just fine, Miss Dixie," I said with a smile.

We caught up for a while. She asked about Father, and I told her he was out of town. She asked me, "Do you know that fella you was just talkin' to?"

"Kinda," I told her.

"Well, it ain't none of my business, but you might want to take care, 'cause Miss Dixie knows for a fact that back in the day, when him and your papa was younger, they tangled. That same Mr. Kohler was the one who give you daddy a fierce whoopin' and left him beat to a pulp on the floor down to Blood's Tavern. All I'm a sayin' is be careful 'cause I knowed your daddy, and I knowed how much he hate that Kohler fella." Miss Dixie informed me of this with great concern.

"Thank you, Miss Dixie; forewarned is forearmed," I told her. We hugged and went about our separate ways.

With that one conversation, Mr. Kohler was elevated onto a pedestal. Short of murder, he was now incapable of taking a wrong step in my mind. The more I thought about him, the better looking he got. Mr. Kohler was the only acceptable choice.

I was up at daybreak and ran all the way to the Florida House. I was bursting at the seams but wanted to wait 'til the right moment to break the good news. Smiling and giggling uncontrollably seemed to raise suspicion around the table, and Lottie and Ava began questioning my rather curious mood.

Then, just like clockwork, Mr. Kohler walked down Columbus Street on his way to work, but this morning as he passed High Street, he looked back over his shoulder and smiled at Miss Caroline. Even at a distance, we all knew exactly who he had glanced at. Lottie and Ava erupted.

"Did you see that? He aimed that smile right at you," Lottie said.

"I can't believe what I just saw," said Ava.

Miss Caroline's cheeks flushed as she held her hand over her mouth, trying to cover a smile.

"And that's not all," I said. "I think he might be coming to supper."

Like a choir, they all chimed in at the same time. "What did you do?"

We sat and talked for over an hour, and I told them every detail of my talk with Mr. Kohler. Miss Caroline was slightly put off that I'd been down in the Bowery after dark, and she made me promise never to do that again. I said yes, but I knew that could be a hard promise to keep with my father back in the picture.

In the event that all would go wrong, for the sake of Miss Caroline, I decided it best to split my time more evenly between Miss Caroline's and Miss Charity's. It would be safer for them and allow me to keep my options open.

"Miss Pearl, you need to keep an eye on Mr. Kohler to find out when he might be coming to supper; that way Ava and I can have Miss Caroline ready to display in all her finery."

I had never seen Miss Caroline so flustered; she blushed every time Lottie or Ava mentioned his name. I was Mr. Kohler's shadow until I knew for sure he was coming to supper.

I left the table and went straight to work keeping an eye on Mr. Kohler. I had already been following him around for a week and found him to be very predictable—up until now. Any anxiety I saw in Miss Caroline paled in comparison to the agony Mr. Kohler was now experiencing.

He left his office on six separate occasions during the course of the day, walking to different locations that offered a distant view of the Florida Boarding House. Here, he would stand lost in thought up to a half hour at a stretch.

What worried me the most was that his lips were moving, but he wasn't uttering a sound. There was no one around whom was he talking to? It was as though he was giving a speech with laryngitis. He'd get the most exasperated look on his face and head back to Customs House, shaking his head in despair. I tell you the truth, if he had been a horse, I'd have shot him just to get him out of his misery. I never would have imagined courting could be so traumatic.

The twelfth was no better. Not only were his lips moving, but now his arms were flailing. He looked like a politician practicing for a speech or perhaps the Vicar just before Sunday service.

He left the office early at three o'clock, and I could tell by the look of resolve on his face, he had committed himself to the fates. I rushed back to inform Lottie and Ava that the time was at hand. Preparations began immediately with no time to spare.

I thought, all in all, this could turn out to be one of my finest days. I now had a potential mother, father, two aunts, and two uncles all picked out. They just didn't know it yet.

Lottie prepared Miss Caroline while Ava and I ran down to the docks to make some last-minute purchases. It was our good fortune that a fishing smack just returned to port, and the red snapper and a flounder were still kicking in the basket on our return home. Ava was weighted down with a half bag of oysters, shrimp, and blue crabs. I went with Ava to the kitchen and began the preparation.

Lottie and Miss Caroline soon joined us. Lottie out did herself, and Miss Caroline was a vision to behold. Much to Miss Caroline's objections, we could not allow her to assist and risk soiling her dress, so she was only allowed to instruct from a safe distance.

The feast that was about to ensue was fit for a king, but Lottie said it needed to appear as though it was like any other day at the restaurant. Just then, Ava came barging threw the swing door into the kitchen.

"He's here. He's coming up the steps," she quietly exclaimed.

Before the kitchen door had time to swing shut, I saw Mr. Kohler standing at the front door surveying the restaurant, and he spotted me. Caught like a deer in a gun sight, all I could do was grin as the door swung shut.

Aggressively encouraged by Lottie and Ava, they practically pushed Miss Caroline through the swinging door into the restaurant. We all stood with our ears to the door, trying to hear what was said, when Lottie suddenly announced, "What are we doing? We have other customers." Ava and I stared, confused at Lottie's words. "We can fill glasses out front where we can hear better," she reminded us.

Grabbing anything we could, we headed out front to check on the other patrons.

I'd have to say Miss Caroline was charming to say the least, but Mr. Kohler was a babbling idiot. I knew from experience he was articulate and able to engage in sparkling conversation, but where was that Mr. Kohler tonight?

When I returned to the kitchen, Lottie saw me scratching my head and asked what was wrong. I told her how Mr. Kohler seemed changed. According to Lottie, it was normal for a smitten man to babble. "It's just the way love works," she assured me.

Smiling, Miss Caroline came back through the swinging door. I was still not sure if I had done her a service or a grievous harm. She grabbed a tray of oysters and went straight back out.

At the time, I felt love must be a strange beast indeed. Miss Caroline, Lottie, and Ava were tickled and felt the evening went well. To me, Mr. Kohler was speaking in tongues. How they extracted from his end of the conversation that he and Miss Caroline had a date for Sunday picnic, I could not fathom. *At the very least*, I thought, *he shouldn't have forgotten to pay his bill.*

Late the next day, Mr. Kohler seemed back to his old self. As a thank you, he presented me with a most personal gift of a sterling silver grooming set and small bottle of perfume that had belonged to his mother. In my life, I would never again receive a gift given with as much love and sincerity as those presented on that day.

***

The Sunday church picnic was the first time I'd ever felt like a part of a family. I had a blanket spread in the church yard and everything ready when Sunday service ended. Mr. Kohler and Miss Caroline insisted that I join them for the day's festivities. Wonderful food and talk, kids playing, and Captain Hatch spinning tales made for a day I only ever dreamed of.

Mr. Kohler began reminiscing about boyhood outings and picnics with his parents long ago. I could see by the look on his face; the church picnic meant as much to him as it did to me. I would never have imagined that a full-grown man like Mr. Michael Brandon Kohler and I could share such a common want and need for a family.

Chapter XV

The War

On the same night we entertained Mr. Kohler at the restaurant, Confederate forces, under the Bonnie Blue Flag, bombarded a place called Fort Sumter in Charleston, South Carolina, and the war officially began. The war had no name. Most just called it "The War." Eventually, some Yankees called it, "War of the Rebellion." In the South, it became known as, "The Terrible War" or "The War for Southern Independence." I soon began to realize what Mr. Kohler was talking about when he spoke with Jacob that day on the dock; nothing was cut and dry. It was as my father, Mr. Kohler, had recorded in his journal.

"War is never noble, and the motives for war are never pure. Men of politics, commerce, and religion driven by the great evils of the world, such as greed and envy, mask the reasons for war, wrapping them in a flag of nobility."

False propaganda played a large role in the patriotic fervor needed to enlist an army. It wasn't until much later that we learned the truth of the great battle at Fort Sumter—not one soul was lost, not really a number worthy for a declaration of war.

Southern politicians found it to the advantage of the Confederate cause to speak of the attack as simply reclaiming that which was ours and letting the people assume the worst had happened. It was an attempt to rally support through Southern pride. In the North, it was the Confederates casting the first stone. It didn't really matter, with or without bloodshed, the truth was we were at war long before Fort Sumter.

It was to my good fortune that Mr. Kohler looked into Miss Caroline's eyes before he knew of the great battle. Wearing the blinders of love and passion, he could better weather the tides of war, pushing through these dark times toward a brighter future, one that hopefully included me.

Things were finally working out as planned. The supper at the Florida House Restaurant, although appearing a little rocky to me, was a great success according to Miss Caroline. A bond formed between me and Mr. Kohler, and he further sealed that bond when he presented me with the most personal gift of his mother's sterling silver grooming set. The church picnic was a gift from God himself and began to bring Mr. Kohler, Miss Caroline, and me together as a family.

Sunday after the picnic, when I arrived back at Miss Charity's, she was still tending to the family. Proud of my new grooming set, I pulled the bag from the wardrobe and laid the assorted pieces out on the table to admire them. Much to my surprise and disdain my father, drunk, barged into the shack. When he saw the silver grooming set, he grabbed them from the table.

"You steal them girl? Ugly little whelp like you don't need nor deserve no fancy brush. You need be gettin' your stuff collected up; we be headin' up to the turpentine camp in a week's time so's I can keep better track of ya'."

"If it would be better for you, I can hitch a ride with the camp supply wagon and just meet you there in a few days," I told him.

"Yeah, that'll be good...." Staggering slightly, he finished by threating me. "But don't be gettin' it your head to be runnin' off like last time, or I'll make sure your friends suffer 'cause of it. You understand me, girl?"

"Yes, Dray. I understand," I scowled back.

He continued to tell me that he and Etta decided that as soon as travel became safe again, we'd be heading over to Pascagoula, Mississippi to meet up with her for the wedding. From there, I'd be returning back to New Orleans with some of my momma's family to spend some time with them. He then turned, vomited in the doorway, and left. I was at a loss, having no idea what to do next. Feeling trapped with no options, I would be forced to travel to the camp to keep my family in Apalachicola out of harm's way.

Miss Charity joined me as I was scrubbing down the porch with a bucket of water, trying to remove all traces of my father's foulness. My mind racing, I blurted out the cause of my distress. She said not to worry and believed everything would work out for the best.

Miss Charity and I sat up late into the night, and she explained to me that there were forces at work beyond what people could see and that the special purpose God had chosen for me was in play. She said I just needed to keep the faith and trust in God, and soon enough, I would receive a great reward. God or not, I was still fearful and lay awake fretting over my father's threats. It was to be a long night.

Unknown to me, at some point during the night, Miss Charity slipped away. Next morning, I awoke to the sound of the Vicar, Ponder, and Miss Charity talking in the front room. Rubbing the cracklings out of my eyes, I joined them, greeting each in turn with a well-deserved hug.

The Vicar opened the conversation with concerns over my father and his growing power in the group calling themselves the Rebel Guard, believing the group of outcasts could soon pose a credible threat. They all agreed with me that I should go the turpentine camp, but they insisted I would need to be accompanied. "Ponder will take you to the camp and stay with you until Miss Charity arrives."

"Miss Charity?" I questioned.

"Yes," said the Vicar. "I spoke with Mr. Orman early this morning and convinced him that he could contribute to the Confederate cause by allowing Charity to make her Pine Tar Soap for our troops. He felt obligated because his son, William, had already enlisted. He would never admit to it, but he was also concerned for his son, John Milton, he and Miss Charity's youngest boy, who was bound to attend to the needs of William Orman throughout his military service.

"We also have an ally at the camp. I received word from Matthew that something our Pearl did had a profound effect on a man named

Elias. Matthew assures me that Elias has been filled with the Holy Spirit and can now be trusted.

"Elias will remain watchful but is helping to keep an eye on the Rebel Guard, so he must remain hidden in the background. His wife and children are now being released from their indentures and will be taken to the Salt Works where they will eventually be reunited. If all goes wrong, I am told you can rely on Elias for help," assured the Vicar. At the time, I couldn't imagine what I did that could have changed Elias, but I was happy for him and his family.

With all that was going on around me, the one thing that plagued my mind the most was how vain I had been. If I had kept Mr. Kohler's gift hidden in the wardrobe instead of admiring myself in the mirror, I would still be in possession of his wonderful gift.

In four days' time at one o'clock, Ponder and I were scheduled to board a steamer and travel up to Brothers River, and from there, we'd follow an old Indian trail and make our way to the turpentine camp. I desperately needed to confess my sins to Mr. Kohler before I left.

How was I going to face Mr. Kohler and tell him I had lost his family treasures? I struggled to come up with a plan, but I was at a loss for words. I found myself avoiding him rather than having to suffer what I thought would be a catastrophe that might separate us forever.

I spent the next couple of days with Miss Caroline and my nights with Miss Charity. Although business was slow at the boarding house, on Wednesday April sixteenth, steamboats arrived from up-river, and once again it was all hands-on deck.

I was running from table to table and even serving meals on the steps out front. Mr. Kohler walked by; he smiled and waved at me, but filled with a sense of dread, I'm afraid my response lacked enthusiasm. I was relieved when he chose to pass by. I was worried, and I could not face him.

I finished my work at the restaurant and hid away in an alley across the street. I sat on a barrel, wrenching my handkerchief around the small bottle of perfume he had given me, the only item that remained from Mr. Kohler's gift. I knew he would be visiting Miss

Caroline this evening, and it would be my last opportunity to explain what happened.

He noticed me as he passed and headed my way. He was very concerned because I seemed so distraught and wanted to know why. I started to explain in a calm voice, but as the first word left my mouth, I fell apart and began blurting out all that happened, hugging him, and begging for his forgiveness.

There was a slight smile on his face as he sat me back up on the barrel, telling me there was nothing to forgive and placing a package in my lap. He told me when I calmed to come over and join him and Miss Caroline on the porch.

The package Mr. Kohler laid on my lap contained the sterling silver grooming set my father stole from me. I could not have known that this very day, Mr. Kohler spotted the grooming set in the window of the pawn broker's shop and purchased it back. It was nothing short of magic and would count as the second time Mr. Kohler had bested my father. I joined them on the porch for the best evening of my life. If I died in my sleep, I would die knowing what it was like to have a mother and father.

***

The day of our departure soon arrived. That morning, I kept busy cleaning rooms and waiting tables, trying to keep my mind off leaving. It was important that Miss Caroline not suspect. I would have walked through fire for Miss Caroline, and I knew she would do the same for me. After my departure, the Vicar would break the news to Miss Caroline that my father had once again taken me away to parts unknown. My heart was breaking knowing I would have to leave without a proper goodbye, as if nothing was wrong.

Everything went as planned, and we arrived at the turpentine camp late evening. Our reception at the company store was less than cordial; one man I didn't recognize introduced us to the foreman as some old nigger strapped with a little white ball and chain.

Foreman James Hancock soon put him in his place when he rose to his feet yelling out, "Pearl, Ponder, come on in and sit down." Ponder kept his head down, but I can assure you that the little, white ball and chain smirked at the boastful, droning, ill-bred lout as she took her seat.

I handed Mr. Hancock a letter from Mr. Thomas Orman addressed, "To whom it may concern." I have to confess that on the trip up, all that steam from the boat's boiler may have loosened the adhesive on the envelope, spilling the content into my hands. I, of course, had to read the letter to put the pages back in order.

The content of the letter was to inform the camp owners that Miss Charity would soon be arriving to make soap for our troops, and Ponder and I were there to prepare the building for her arrival. Mr. Orman made it very clear, he expected us to receive every courtesy they could afford. He stated in the letter that he hoped the small building to the northeast of the still would be made available for her to perform her duties.

Mr. Orman may not have owned the still or the two hundred acres of land it sat on, but he did own and profit from the collection of resin and the lumber from 39,000 acres of pine trees surrounding it. The turpentine camp was an island, sitting in the middle of Thomas Orman's ocean of Long Leaf Pines.

Father, having been absent for months, had his own agenda. What he was up to, I had no idea, but I suspected it was no good. He had given Foreman Hancock some money and placed me in camp as an indentured servant, expecting me to pay my way by working in the kitchen, cleaning bunk houses, and helping out at the camp laundry. This internment served my father well; it was the camp's responsibility to keep me in check and work me like any other indentured servant. My father could then easily retrieve me at his leisure and collect the bounty by returning me to my mother's family, but what my father didn't know was that I arrived with a letter from Mr. Orman.

Mr. Hancock was pleased when he read the letter from Mr. Orman that included me as one of his workers. Mr. Hancock allowed Miss Charity and me to use my father's money to purchase a few little extras to make our stay more tolerable.

After grabbing a bite to eat at the company store, we headed down to the soap works building and set up camp. It was to be another troubled night as my mind raced trying to make sense of it all.

To me, slit throats and murder were just a part of growing up. I used to believe it must be a common way to die, but after reading old issues of the *Advertiser*, I realized how uncommon it was.

Bella and Mrs. Freud were not the first people I had seen or known to be killed by this method. Over the years, I picked the pockets of many people who suffered the same fate. I can remember my father from the seat of the wagon, instructing me on how best to pickpocket the dead.

I shudder to think how normal it used to feel. These days, I would liken my father to a vulture teaching its young to feed on carrion. Even if it was obvious by their skin that they suffered from the Yellow Fever, it would still have been considered murder to hasten their deaths to rob them.

Yellow Fever claimed countless victims up and down the coastline. Oppressive heat and damp generated the swamp gasses that spread the Yellow Fever. Trying to avoid contagion, families fled to the woods searching for areas where they believed the air was pure. It was here in some lovely patch of the forest we would find their bodies. After an outbreak, we would look for their camps and hopefully find the victims still fresh, their skin yellow and covered with blue patches. It was good to find sites where the wild hogs had not yet found the bodies. Then began the search for their treasures; they always took their most valuable possessions with them in hopes that one person would survive. We looked for disturbed earth because the last person, sick and dying, would be the one who buried the family treasure.

I now realized that slit throats were uncommon and the signature of a single killer, a signature I feared was that of my father.

Contemplating murder at my age was a hard row to hoe, but it was my row. I kept telling myself he must be stopped, and I had no intention of going anywhere with him. For me, it was just a matter of figuring out how and when.

I slept late, joining Ponder by the cook fire around six as the sun began to light the horizon. Ponder, already having prepared breakfast, kept it warm in the Dutch oven off to the side of the fire.

Morning fires were my favorite. Warm and toasty and with a blanket over my shoulders, I held it open in front so the heat of the fire warmed me all around. The morning mist couldn't penetrate the heat given off by the bed of coals still glowing red from the night before. It wouldn't be long before the fire would lose its appeal to the oppressive heat of summer. Early morning was a quiet time when the predators of the night were tucked away, and the creatures of light began to stir. In the mist at the edge of the forest, I made out the form of a small herd of deer, and intermingled among them, a flock of wild turkeys scratched at the grass looking for their breakfast. Ponder had something on his mind and was struggling to put his thoughts into words.

"What's the matter, Ponder?" I asked.

"Miss Pearl, I's gots somethin' I has to tell you that gonna make me seem a might ungrateful for all you done for Old Ponder, but I gots to tell yah."

Ponder had been free long enough that he was starting to feel a sense of duty. He told me, "The talk going around is that them Yankees, they gonna free all the slaves."

Ponder wanted to be a part of their freedom. He had it in his mind that when the first Yankee steamer showed up off Apalachicola, he wanted to join them and help liberate all the people still held in bondage. I was so proud of him. With tears in my eyes, unable to speak, I hugged him; it was with a strangled voice I whispered in his ear, "I will miss you."

***

Miss Charity arrived mid-May, and we started producing soap. Mr. Orman made sure we received our supplies on a regular basis. Ponder crated the soap we produced and stacked it on the camp wagons between the barrels of rosin. Heading north, the wagon made its way up the Apalachee Trail to the Confederate River blockade at the Narrows, and there the cargo was loaded onto steamers for the journey up river.

Eighteen sixty-one was a frightening year along the Gulf Coast, not because of military engagements, but rather because of the lack of credible information. The rumor mills had everyone stirred up. It was reported that the Yankees were enlisting Hessian mercenaries to burn and pillage Southern ports. The *USS Montgomery*, just passing by, was enough to make otherwise reasonable people panic and flee for cover.

Naval Stores, rosin, and turpentine were crucial to the building of a Confederate Navy. The rosin melted down and mixed with hemp fibers was used to seal the hulls of war ships. So important was turpentining to the war effort that all turpentine camp workers were exempt from military service in order to keep the camps producing.

I held onto hope, reflecting the feelings of many; I prayed the war would be short lived and I'd soon be returning to Apalachicola, but it was not meant to be. On July twenty-first in 1861, at a battle called Manassas, it became apparent it would be a long and costly war.

Apalachicola had gone silent, I was in agony because I did not know the status of Mr. Kohler's and Miss Caroline's budding relationship. Miss Charity didn't seem to be worried at all. She still firmly believed that unseen forces were at work and a favorable outcome lay at the end of my journey.

Chapter XVI

The Devils Own

I liken the smell of his breath to soured milk and his body to that of a maggot infested carcass on a hot day. His weight pushing me into the ground rendered me helpless as he lay across my back ripping at my dress.

***

It was just after dark when I returned to camp with a bag of salt I had fetched for Miss Charity. Supper was simmering in the pot, and I smelled it as I walked down the path to the Soap Works. The fire burned brightly on the far side of the Soap Works and illuminated the outline of the building. A candle burning in the window gave it a warm and cozy look.

Look hard enough, and beauty can be found in unexpected places. With the war heating up, it looked as though we might be here for a while. I was resolved to make the best of my current situation. Between the three of us, the old Soap Works was starting to look rather homey, not such a bad place to wait out a war.

I always looked forward to sitting around the fire listening to Miss Charity and Ponder reminisce. Ponder talked about how he and his Miss Millie raised me from a pup, tellin' his stories of all the orneriness I got into as baby and a small child.

He'd start funnin' 'n pokin' at me, trying to get a reaction, telling me how cantankerous I used to be. I couldn't remember most of what he was talking about, but pretty soon, I'd start pokin' back, funning him anyway, telling him I was a perfect angel and how he should be honored to have raised a perfect little princess like me.

Tonight would be very different; as I approached the shack, a foul odor fell upon me. I had smelled it before but couldn't place it. As I came around the side of the building into the light of the fire, I saw Ponder lying face down on the ground near the soap kettle. I started for him, but a noise beyond the fire caught my attention, and I held my hands up, trying to shade the fire light so I might better peer into the shadows.

A camp wagon had been sitting there for a week with a busted axel, but tonight, there was something new. As I approached the edge of the fire, I began to make out the pattern on Miss Charity's dress. She was crouched on her knees, her hands were bound with leather straps to the back wheel, and her head was covered with a canvas sack.

I started to run to her when I was tackled from behind and forced to the ground. Suddenly, I recognized the smell. It was Aldridge. "'Member me girly? I come to make you a woman. This be a lucky night fer ya."

I couldn't even scream; his weight crushed the air from my lungs. He gagged me with a rag and continued to rip at my clothes. When my back was bare, I could feel him probing with his hand and cock, trying to gain entry.

I had never been so helpless and screamed, *"Please God!"* over and over again in my mind.

God is a force to be reckoned with. In Revelations, God called on the archangel Michael to go to war, and in God's name, Michael defeated the devil himself.

As quickly as the assault had begun, it ended. A great shadow fell over me as I struggled to free myself, and suddenly Aldridge was simply gone. I pulled the rag from my mouth and crawled over to Miss Charity, pulling the bag from her head and untying her hands. She hugged me tightly, removing the outer layer of her skirt which she wrapped around me.

We stared toward the sound of cracking boards. Rising to our feet, we circled around the opposite side of the fire. Making our way over to Ponder, Miss Charity assessed the extent of Ponder's injury. I stood in shock unable to move, watching as my archangel, Elias, bashed Aldridge repeatedly into the side of the building, shattering the cypress board siding. In a blinding rage, Elias raised Aldridge into the air above his head and carried him out to the fire. Old Hickory could not have matched the bellowing from Elias as he threw Aldridge face down into the fire. Elias was far from finished and began stomping him into the hot coals.

Running to Elias, I pulled at his shirt screaming, "Elias look at me! I'm here. I'm all right!" Elias, with his mind consumed in darkness, peered down upon me with a look that could have split stone. Suddenly, his face changed, and he picked me up and carried me to Miss Charity. He placed me in her embrace then cradled Ponder in his arms. He carried him into the shack and lay him on my cot.

The commotion alerted the camp, and men were running down the path to see what was happening. I looked back to the fire, but Aldridge was gone. The foreman, James Hancock, soon arrived yelling, "What the hell is going on?"

Miss Charity spoke out. "Ponder's been injured."

Mr. Hancock quickly ordered the camp doctor to attend to Ponder and asked Elias to speak his mind. "A man was tryin' to have his way with our Miss Pearl, and I stopped him!" said Elias.

Mr. Hancock reached up placing his hand on Elias' chest, trying to calm him. He turned to the crew and in a commanding voice ordered, "Get the hounds, boys. Heat up the tar. I want this man found and feathered by morning. If that don't get it done, we gonna have us a hangin'."

Turning back to Elias, he tried to get him to calm down. "You done good Elias; you done real good. I want you to come over by the fire, and we'll have a look at you. Yah hurt?" James asked.

"Nah, he's a little fella. Weren't no trouble."

"Yah got some blood on yer mouth Elias. You sure you didn't on accident swallow that fella?" James asked. Men standing around Elias started chuckling and patting him on the back, and they led him out to the fire. Mr. Hancock was wise to lighten the mood. Elias was a mountain of a man and needed to know that he was being listened to.

It pleased me and gave me some comfort when Mr. Hancock yelled, "Heat up the tar." History recorded that Spaniards captured by the Aztecs and Incas were made to drink molten gold as punishment for their greed. The hot liquid exploded organs and bowels as it scorched its way through the gut and back out of the body.

The equivalent in the South was tar and feathers. Sometimes, the resin was left to cool and the feathers applied just to humiliate for a wrong deed. For more severe crimes, the resin was brought to boil and poured on the criminal, causing them to cook in a sticky amber-colored shell. Very few survived after having their skin seared off from a hot tarring. It would be a fitting end for a bastard like Aldridge, but at this moment, even death would fall short of satisfying me.

The camp doctor walked out of the shack and spoke with Miss Charity. I quickly headed in and held Ponder's hand. The doctor did a fine job tending to the wound on his head where Aldridge struck him with that shovel.

***

Next morning, the best we could figure, Aldridge must have had a boat anchored up and escaped down the Brothers River. Otherwise, with the way he smelled, he couldn't have gotten away from the hounds.

Ponder remained unconscious for three days. Miss Charity and I took turns, never once leaving him unattended. We fed him broth so he might keep up his strength. On the third day, he awoke and seemed fine, but he wasn't fine, and over the next two weeks, his condition deteriorated.

Ponder began to lose control of his right side. It was as though he was split in half, one half no longer obeying his commands. Miss

Charity had seen this before and called it by the name, "Severe Brain Attack." Much to my dismay, Ponder faded into a dream and passed away the last Sunday of October 1861.

Miss Charity and I picked a nice spot down by the Brothers River, under a live oak, to lay Ponder to rest. Miss Charity wept; she had become very fond of Ponder. I knew she was holding back her pain, trying to be strong on account of me.

September and October of 1861 marked one of the saddest chapters of my life. I don't think I will ever really recover from the events that transpired. To this day, my dreams are haunted by the pain and loss we experienced at the hands of one evil man.

I once listened to a dramatic reading, and although I cannot remember the name of the author or the text, I do remember the orator's words: "Wherever God erects a house of prayer, The Devil always builds a chapel there: And 'twill be found, upon examination, the latter has the largest congregation."

When the fear of God leaves a man, the devil finds fertile ground on which to build his chapel. The Vicar used to call it a moral compass, the voice inside that helps you to distinguish that which is right from the unthinkable.

People who lost their moral compass were typically loners, plying their obsessions against the unsuspecting and then hiding themselves away in the shadows to avoid detection. Although looking like everyone else, their twisted minds and lack of conscience made them dangerous predators.

In extraordinary times, these loners formed into packs to increase their chance of survival. There was power in the pack, and so, unholy alliances were formed. It was in this time of war that such a pack was formed and given a misleading name, "The Rebel Guard."

***

After Ponder's death, I fell into a deep depression. Every night, I woke screaming from the demons that now lived in my mind. Miss

Charity was there to comfort me, but she didn't have the words to make the pain go away.

The second week of December 1861, found me sitting down by the edge of the Brothers River near Ponder's grave. I sat thinking of Ponder as I threw sticks into the water watching them float downstream. Ponder was the first man who ever really cared for me; he was my first father.

I imagined him in a Yankee blue uniform, valiantly fighting to liberate all those enslaved. I did the math and couldn't hardly believe that Ponder was an old man near sixty. The only thing I could figure was that when I looked at him, all I ever saw was his spirit, and Ponder's spirit was that of a much younger man. Had he lived, Ponder would have made a noble and magnificent soldier.

I was suddenly awakened from my daydream by the sound of Miss Charity's voice yelling down to me from the seat of a camp wagon. "What you doin' child?"

"Nothin', Miss Charity; just sittin'," I answered.

"All dis important sittin' you doin', I's don't 'magin you knowed that Captain Hatch was just in camp."

"No ma'am," I answered.

She knew good and well that she had peaked my interest. There didn't seem to be a woman alive who didn't feel a grin coming on at the mention of his name. "What did he want, Miss Charity?" I asked.

"He come with all kind of news from Apalachicola." Miss Charity knew if she remained quiet, it would force me to speak.

"What kind of news, Miss Charity?"

"Oh, the kind of news like Mr. Kohler done gone and proposed marriage to that Miss Caroline, and she done accepted."

She knew she had me. I was about to bust right out of my seams. I started running toward the wagon hollering out, "When they gettin' married, Miss Charity?"

"Well, they seem to be waitin' for a young lady to get back to town 'fore they tie dat knot. You knowed who they talkin' about?"

I held a smile behind my hands and replied, "They talkin' about me, Miss Charity."

"Well, I feel much the same. I kinda thinkin' they talkin' 'bout you too. How 'bout you climb up, and I just tell you what else Miss Charity knows."

We traveled back to camp, and Miss Charity told me all the news from Apalachicola. This would be the first night in over a month I would lay awake because of something joyous rather than tragic. It wasn't until next day by the morning fire when she told me about the war and how it would further delay our return, but not even the war could dampen my spirits over the engagement and the fact that I had not been forgotten.

Allen & Thurber Pepperbox

After the attack and tragic death of Ponder, Elias became my new protector. He felt I needed to be better equipped to fend off attackers, so he presented me with a small Pepperbox. I thanked him for the gun and swore him to secrecy to keep Miss Charity from knowing of the gift. On occasions, we slipped away from the camp, and Elias taught me how to shoot.

It was a small gun made by a company called Allen & Thurber, twenty-eight caliber, six shot, with a three-inch revolving barrel. You would turn the barrel from hole to hole to fire a new chamber. I was sure they called it a Pepperbox because when looking at the end of the barrel, the six holes made it look like a pepper shaker. It was easy to fire, even for me, except sometimes, the spark from firing one chamber would ignite other chambers, so it was hard to tell how many chambers might fire at the same time. But that was okay because when I would eventually spill the brains of my father and Aldridge, the more barrels, the merrier.

***

In December 1861, and January 1862, I prayed for the deliverance of my beloved town. Apalachicola was abandoned by the new Confederate government. The large cannons brought over from Pensacola to protect the town were removed from the battery at the mouth of the river and from West Pass at St. Vincent Island. My town would soon be defenseless and at the mercy of the Yankee's Hessian mercenaries.

Down the Atlantic coastline, Southern ports were under siege by a rapidly growing Union Navy. Well-equipped and looking for a fight, the Union Navy would soon round the Keys and spread like the Yellow Fever, infecting the Gulf waters.

It was December twenty-first when a handful of our Confederate boys passed through camp heading north to the Narrows. They confirmed that on the sixteenth the *USS Hatteras* was spotted lying off St. Vincent Island near the site of the dismantled battery. When they observed the Yankees using the Cape St. George lighthouse to spy on the town, our Confederate boys slipped in and burned the interior staircase.

Under new orders, they moved north to the stronghold being established at Ricko's Bluff, ninety miles up-river from the Gulf. My hope was that supplies would still be allowed to flow down the river from the North, or Apalachicola could starve to death.

A later report told of the *USS Mercedita* launching a cutter and whaler filled with well-armed troops who landed in Apalachicola—no reports of shots fired, just of talk and terms.

It wasn't until April third that the siege became official. The gunboat *USS Sagamore* launched eight armed boats and captured all remaining vessels in the bay and port. After all the talk, I hardly believed that to this point, it had remained bloodless. The town was taken with no resistance. I began to question the reports of Hessians bent on destruction.

Chapter XVII

No Exceptions

There is just no way to sugar coat the fact that politicians lie. Politicians say whatever, to whomever, in order to get elected. Once in office, they do what they want. Mr. Lincoln was no different. The war started over secession and state's rights and was in transition as Mr. Lincoln changed the focus to the emancipation of the slaves. Looking back, I think it was his intention the whole time.

In August of 1861, the northern congress passed the confiscation act. Slaves used to support the Confederate war effort were given the status of "contraband" and seized. Before the contraband act, depending on the Union commander, some slaves were returned to their masters if those masters could prove their loyalty to the United States. After March of 1862, a new article was passed forbidding the return of any fugitive slave to their master.

"Them Yanks, they started whistling "Yankee Doodle" whilst they commenced to bustin' everthin' up, everthin' lest it would burn; then they lit it on fire," was reported by a passing Confederate soldier. It wasn't until a family from the Salt Works passed through heading north that I would learn the whole truth.

It was my former teacher from the Salt Works who informed us that in the first week of September 1861, a landing party from the *USS Kingfisher* under Lt. Commander Couthouy landed at St. Joseph Bay. Under a flag of truce, they approached my Salt Works at Cape San Blas. Boss Clay met with them and was informed that the production of salt must immediately desist, and all slaves would be removed before the destruction of the works.

Boss Clay informed Lt. Couthouy that the works held no slaves and that all residents of the Salt Works were free men claiming this place as their home. He asked that they be allowed to continue, but his request was refused. All Southern Salt Works were to be destroyed in an attempt to cripple the Confederate forces ability to preserve food.

His plea to continue to make salt for the civilian population was also ignored. He was finally told that orders were orders. He still protested but realized that this commander was going to blindly obey his orders with no exceptions.

Knowing a small contingent of Confederate troops lay three miles inland placed Boss Clay square in the middle of a very bad situation. He tried to shut down the camp, but many didn't believe that if they would but remain peacefully, the Union might change their minds and pass by.

While some placed themselves under the protection of the Union Navy for relocation, others stayed and continued firing the kettles night and day, hoping beyond hope that the commander of the *Kingfisher* might reconsider.

On September 8th, 1862, The *USS Kingfisher* pulled into St. Joseph Bay making its way to within a quarter mile of the Salt Works. Twenty, heavily armed men approached the Salt Works through the trees and held position just outside camp. Realizing what was happening, the remaining families loaded wagons with whatever they could grab and headed inland at a furious pace. To their credit, the Union held their position for two hours before lobbing a few shells into the Salt Works. Then surrounding the Salt Works, the soldiers began whistling "Yankee Doodle" as they began their destructive task.

I was heartbroken that the little bastion of freedom we worked so hard to create was, in two hours' time, nothing more than rubble and cinders. And to what purpose—some unseen greater good?

Destruction of the Salt Works by the bark *USS Kingfisher*.

Soon, no force on earth would prevent me from returning to my beloved Apalachicola.

Captain Hatch returned to the camp toward the end of November. Miss Charity did all the talking, and although he didn't acknowledge me, I felt as though he might have recognized me from the trip I took on the *River Bride*. When we were ready to leave, Miss Charity mentioned me by name, and Captain Hatch perked up, looking at me as though I were a loose coin rolling on a deck.

Captain Hatch left the camp but returned in a fortnight and upon arrival headed straight down the path to the Soap Works. I spotted him coming and quickly ran inside to brush my hair—why I felt the need to brush my hair I don't know. Listening from inside, I'll be darned if he didn't ask Miss Charity if he could speak to me.

I apprehensively walked out to join the conversation. "Hello, Miss Pearl," he said with a charismatic smile, and of course, for no good reason, I became speechless and giggled.

Little did I know that on his previous visit, Captain Hatch recognized me and made the connection between myself and Mr. Kohler. According to him, Mr. Kohler was pining, missing me something fierce. As a matter of fact, he and Miss Caroline put the wedding on hold until I returned.

Captain Hatch said that Mr. Kohler was to the point that he would either have to put him down like a lame horse or arrange for a reunion. I was overjoyed that he chose the latter; our reunion would be on January eleventh.

He also told us that Mr. Lincoln, as early as September of this year, sent out a proclamation that stipulated if the South didn't cease their rebellion by January 1, 1863, his Emancipation Proclamation would pass into law, thereby freeing all slaves held in rebellious states. It was very good news about the slaves being freed, but at eight years old, I'd have to admit I was much more excited about Mr. Kohler's visit.

Miss Charity and I celebrated Christmas as best we could under the circumstances. We all knew if the Union figured it was important to destroy the Salt Works, they'd soon make their way up-river into the interior to find us and destroy the turpentine still. These were unnerving times as everyone kept looking over their shoulders.

***

Captain Hatch wasn't even out of sight before I began making plans for Mr. Kohler's visit. Not wanting him to think I was a jinx, I made Miss Charity promise to keep all the tragic events of the past year a secret.

Miss Charity said I could stay up all night and visit with Mr. Kohler, so I decided I'd be needing quite a bit of fire wood. I spent two days collecting a formidable pile of wood. I'd swipe some at night from the pile at the still, and while the men were out working, I'd swipe a little from their piles, but not so much that they'd notice. Elias commented, "Woo wee! Miss Pearl, that's a mighty pile o' wood you got there."

According to Captain Hatch, Mr. Kohler was due to arrive the afternoon of Sunday the eleventh. I was up early pestering Miss Charity to get the stew simmering early. I knew for a fact that the longer it simmered, the more flavorsome it became.

I did not know at the time, but Captain Hatch kept me a secret from Mr. Kohler, wanting me to be a surprise, and surprised he was as I came running up, threw off my hat, and leaped into his arms. Throwing him off balance, I knocked him flat on his back, and there on the ground we reveled in each other's company. He yelled out in celebration. It was a wonderful reunion; he was so happy to see me.

I sat on his chest, patting his cheeks, and it was in that moment I became enlightened. When I first saw Mr. Kohler walking down the street back in Apalachicola, I couldn't understand what it was Miss Caroline and the girls saw that made him so special. He was unusually tall and appeared to be crippled. He was not the prettiest man I had ever seen by a long shot. I puzzled why Miss Caroline blushed at the mention of his name—but in that moment, looking into his eyes, I saw it. I saw what it was that made Miss Caroline blush.

What I experienced was a gentle kindness and sincerity that touched me to my soul. The man was filled with the grace of God and didn't realize it. Mr. Kohler was perhaps the kindest, most virtuous man anyone could have the privilege of loving, and to have him love me back was an honor I would fight for. I wanted so badly to cry out, Father, Father.

From that moment on, although unspoken, Michael Brandon Kohler was my father, and I could tell by the look in his eyes, he claimed me as his child. It was the most profound experience of my life.

I took him around camp, showing him all of my haunts. I'm afraid, in my excitement, I continuously talked, not allowing Mr. Kohler to get a word in edgewise, but as I jabbered on, he was smiling and shaking his head with an unmistakable look of pride in his eyes. He was proud of me; as with my mother I was his little Pearl.

The visit ended all too abruptly when I fell asleep at eleven thirty. Waking next morning, I discovered Mr. Kohler had already left to meet Captain Hatch at the Narrows. Miss Charity told me not to be upset. We were also leaving this very day, and, after one brief stop would soon be back in Apalachicola.

The Confederates blockaded the river expecting an attack from the Gulf. The main blockade was at Ricko's Bluff, but blockades were also manned at Fort Gadsden, The Narrows, Alum Bluff, and Hammock Landing.

Miss Charity felt the Yankees would soon be headed our way to shut down the still and liberate the slaves. It didn't really matter that the Yankees were coming, the Confederate Command decided to close down the last channels that allowed the shipment of rosin north to the shipyards. The camp would soon be out of business anyway. Unfortunately, it also meant supplies could no longer reach Apalachicola from the North. I was concerned.

For safety, Miss Charity made plans for us to move down river to a more secure location. Her son Matthew waited for us at the end of our journey and would determine the safest way back into Apalachicola. Elias would accompany us down river. His family waited with Matthew and anxiously looked forward to a reunion.

The plan was to float down the Apalachicola River to just north of Apalachicola where we'd pick up the Jackson River and head west to Lake Wimico. Our destination was Depot Creek on the south side of the lake. The lake was shallow, really more of a bayou than a lake and was of no strategic interest to the Union. It was hard enough to float a skiff without hitting a stump or becoming logged in the muck; the larger Union boat wouldn't stand a chance.

Before the Yellow Fever outbreak of 1841, when St. Joseph was still on the map, Depot Creek was a hub of activity. Back then, the lake channel was dredged, and Depot Creek was where the steamboats gathered to transfer cargo to Florida's first steam railway. It was the steam locomotive that carried the cotton the last nine miles directly to the wharfs of St. Joseph.

The Confederates weren't the only ones blockading the river. We were cautioned by many to avoid Forbes Island. The Rebel Guard, led by my father, used Forbes Island as their base, sending raiding parties inland and ambushing unsuspecting boats traveling the river. They claimed they were scavenging supplies in the name of the Confederacy, but they were, in fact, just a pack of pirates and highwaymen.

We were told it was safer to pass by in late evening, hugging the eastern shore of the Apalachicola River. The glow of the nightly cook fires served to give away the location of their camp inside the tree line on the north end of the river island.

Thirty-five miles north of the bay, the Apalachicola River splits forming a river island—Forbes Island. On the west side of Forbes Island, the river was given a new name, Brothers River while the Apalachicola continued north along the east side. The rivers rejoined just above Fort Gadsden at the Brickyard Cutoff near the "Log Jam." From here, the Brothers River turned heading northwest toward the turpentine camp and the Apalachicola continued north.

If not for the fact that it was an island, one could get lost on Forbes Island. The Island was near ten thousand acres and within its borders flowed the Little Brothers, Harrison, Bearman, and Smokehouse Creeks. It was easy, at times, to become disoriented.

We hoped to pass by the Rebel Guard's camp late evening and spend the night down river at the Confederate camp at Fort Gadsden, but just before leaving, we were informed that the fever was paying a visit at Gadsden. We chose instead to set our sights further down river to the small island at Bloody Bluff.

I proceeded around camp to say goodbye to my friends and wish them well. I stopped last at the camp store to let Mr. Hancock know we were leaving and to offer him many thanks for making our stay so tolerable.

During our conversation, I couldn't help but notice a most curious paper on his desk. I wouldn't have noticed it at all, buried among the scattered papers, but on this particular paper was a drawing, my drawing. I asked if I might see the paper, and he was very obliging, handing me one of the four copies he planned to post around camp.

The notice came from the Marshal's Office in Columbus, Georgia. On the notice was a rendering of my drawing of Old Hickory and below it the words, Gator Rosin. Mr. Hancock became concerned as I agonized over the document.

"What is it Pearl?" he asked.

"I know these children…" and I began weeping uncontrollably.

Mr. Hancock quickly sent a man to bring Miss Charity. Unable to speak, I laid the poster on his desk and wrote the names Odila and Zelig Freud, Bainbridge, Mr. Fredric Freud, Freud Mill Work Supply.

At a boat works in Columbus, the bodies of two children were found in the bottom of a rosin barrel encased in amber. The barrel was marked with my drawing and the words, Gator Rosin.

By the time Miss Charity arrived, I was no longer crying. I was angry. Darkness took over my mind, and I was absolute in my resolve. It was now between me and the Rebel Guard. I knew the best way to kill a snake was to cut off its head. My father, Dray, had to die. I was reminded of a passage, and I whispered it aloud:

> "And I looked, and behold a pale horse: and his name that sat on him was Death, and Hell followed with him. And power was given unto them over the fourth part of the earth, to kill with sword, and with hunger, and with death, and with the beasts of the earth."
> Revelation 6:8

Although small, I was determined to bring the fires of Hell down on the heads of those responsible for bringing great evil among us.

I knew it was a sin to seek vengeance, but God was working too slowly to suit me. I wanted retribution for the deaths of Bella, Basher, Ponder, Odila, Ida, Mr. Freud, and Zelig and was anxious to place these evil men in judgment before the throne of God. And if God were to judge me evil by thought or action, I was willing to accept my place in Hell beside my enemies. My only vindication might have to be that no one else would die by their hands.

I knew Miss Charity and Elias were concerned over my state of mind. I pushed them to finish our preparations; I wanted to leave as soon as possible. Miss Charity was puzzled when I asked Elias to load a small barrel of turpentine into the wagon. I simply explained it was a surprise for my father.

We made our way by wagon down to the Brothers River and from there by skiff to just shy of the Brickyard Cutoff. Here, we would wait until we saw the glow of the Rebel Guard's cook fires on the north end of Forbes Island.

A near full moon started to rise as we made our way onto the river. A stout south wind was a godsend and served well to keep us cool and those pesky skeeters at bay.

The south wind soon played an important role in a very dark plan I was orchestrating in my mind. The speed and direction were made to order and seemed too perfect to be coincidental. I took it as a sign that God might still be on my side.

Against Miss Charity's objections, I made Elias row onto Forbes Island just across from the Smith Creek Landing. I knew the island formed a slight bottleneck at the end of Bearman Creek. We were less than a mile from the Rebel Guard's camp, so we needed to proceed with caution. A hunting trail crossed the island at this point, and with a bright moon, we proceeded without the use of a lantern or torches.

Forbes Island was heavily forested. Below a canopy of long leaf pines, tupelo, and water oaks lie a tangle of yaupon, wax myrtle, palmetto, and Spanish bayonets. With so much ground clutter, it was difficult to walk even a short distance into the wood. Without the trail, it was easiest to row around the island than to cross it on foot.

Elias followed me onto the island, toting the turpentine barrel on his shoulder. When we reached the Brothers River, I told Elias to tap the barrel and spill its content along the north side of the path back across the island to the skiff. With the Apalachicola River in sight, I fired a torch and set the north end of Forbes Island on fire.

I had been told that to escape a fire up north, one should run toward the green, but in the south, that was bad advice. Our plants were filled with oil and burned with hell's fury. Before we could reach the skiff, the wind pushed the fire up the vines into the canopy. There were now two fires, one on the ground and a much faster moving fire in the canopy. Both headed directly for the Rebel Guard's camp.

Elias pushed off from shore, and the current carried us away. Even with a strong wind at my back, I felt the heat of the fire on my face. In a matter of minutes, the Guard would be consumed in flames. I would be surprised if, at the very least, the Guard didn't lose most of their booty and supplies. As I record this tale, I can hardly believe I was ever so callous, but at the time, I prayed the fire would take their lives.

Miss Charity waited in the boat, and I could tell by her face, she was worried. Although the fire was contained to the north end of Forbes Island, aimed at my father, she was more troubled by the fire burning in my soul. She had plans for my future family, and my anger and hate could put those plans in jeopardy.

A bright moon and star-filled night convinced us to pass by Bloody Bluff and continue down river. Miss Charity passed out bread and jerky to satisfy our hunger and told old stories to try and lighten the mood. I was still finding great satisfaction in the glow of the fire to the north. Elias jerked when far up-river an explosion startled him. "Sounds like black powder to me Miss Pearl," he said with a smile.

It was early morning when we reached the mouth of the Jackson River. Elias pulled the oars and set them in the locks, rowing us up-stream and west toward Lake Wimico. We pulled up on shore just shy of the Jackson River Ford to get a couple hours sleep before we continued on.

This was the hardest part of the journey for me because I knew the ford in the river was the Apalachee Trail, and from the ford I could easily walk and be in Apalachicola within two hours. It was all Miss Charity could do to convince me to trust her and follow the safer path. The sun soon stood testament to her wisdom.

***

When I woke, Miss Charity signaled me to keep quiet. Moving closer to the river, we peeked up-stream toward the ford. Wagons full of Yankee soldiers were fording the river, moving inland up the Apalachee Trail. It was an impressive sight with all the blue uniforms and the clanking of rifles and sabers. Many were Negroes, but they carried no weapons. Negroes were tasked with hauling equipment and driving the wagons. I thought of Ponder and how handsome he'd have been in one of those fancy, blue uniforms.

Union blockaders ford the Jackson River.

***

Elias, on reconnoiter, was just making his way back through the wood to join us by the river. He reported to Miss Charity that she was right; the town was crawling with Union soldiers. The Union blockade dispatched several heavily-armed Whalers rowing up-river.

He got close enough to hear their plans. They were heading upstream to Orman's Owl Creek Plantation and the turpentine camp with every intention of liberating slaves and destroying the still. The plan was to travel up the Brothers River avoiding Fort Gadsden and stay below the Narrows to avoid a conflict with the Confederates at the river obstruction.

It was with God's intervention that we had navigated the river at night and found ourselves in a safe camp along the Jackson River. If we had been discovered, they would have separated us, sending Miss Charity south to the Keys with the rest of the Orman slaves where they were told by the Union they would find work in agriculture. Elias might find himself imprisoned as a Confederate. For the most part, I was an orphan; it was hard to tell where I would have wound up.

We remained encamped until Elias determined that it was safe to move on. It was about two o'clock when we continued on our journey west, rowing toward the lake. It wasn't all that far, and Miss Charity and I kept close watch for any sign of trouble. By four o'clock, we were on Lake Wimico, and before five, we were pulling into an encampment at Depot Creek.

We sensed we were being watched from shore from the time we entered the lake to when we pulled up at Depot Creek. It came as no surprise when Elias's wife and children came running to greet him. Matthew gave his momma a big hug and hoisted me into the air. Everyone was celebrating our safe arrival.

Of those who gathered, I recognized many of the faces from the Salt Works. After the Union destroyed the Salt Works, they fled to this remote outpost in the hopes of waiting out the war. The fishing and hunting were good enough to feed the twenty-five to thirty people, who at times called this place home. Winter vegetable gardens produced a variety of cabbage and greens to supplement the diet of fish, turtle, squirrel, bear, deer, hog, and gator.

Except for the news of a fever outbreak at Fort Gadsden, we were lucky not to have had a major outbreak since the war began. All things considered, this was not a bad place to hide as the rest of our world descended into madness.

Chapter XVIII

Darkness & Light

It would be the Minie Ball and Iron Clads which changed the face of war. The terror of being bested in battle and dying in hand to hand combat was once the greatest deterrent to war. I was disheartened to think there were men whose sole purpose in life was to come up with more efficient ways of killing people.

With a Minie Ball and riffled barrel, accuracy increased to two-hundred-fifty yards. From the stories coming off the battlefields, a bullet entering the brain or heart was preferred over suffering the damage when lead shattered against bone, sending shards ravaging through a man's body. Amputated arms and legs marked the entrance of battlefield hospitals, piled high outside surgery tent flaps.

According to reports coming out of Tennessee, the number of men falling in battle paled in comparison to those dying from diseases with names like Dysentery, Pneumonia, Measles, Tuberculosis, and Malaria. How could leaders on both sides be so blinded by hate that they did not see they were losing the war to a greater unseen enemy? Man's inhumanity to man never ceased to amaze me.

Soon after arriving at Depot Creek, Miss Charity, once again, began to suffer from her decrepitude, and for the next few weeks, I turned my attention to her care. Miss Charity asked Matthew to sit with me and explain about old age, dying, and heaven. I tried to assure him he had nothing to worry about, and that under my care, his momma would soon be back to her old self.

I could tell Elias was having second thoughts about giving me the Pepperbox. I think Matthew and Miss Charity found me out and had something to do with his change of heart. Whenever we started out in the wood to practice, we'd end up fishing or just taking a walk.

In his eyes, I was a pure spirit. He gave me the gun for protection. It was my attack against the Rebel Guard on Forbes Island that offered confirmation of the murderous intent festering inside of me. I could tell he was worried about giving me the gun in the first place.

I worked out a variety of scenarios, but I dwelled on one in particular. There was an alley beside Blood's Tavern where men went to relieve themselves. They stood by a stack of old crates that shielded them from onlookers.

I intended to hide myself in those crates, and when Dray or Aldridge presented themselves, I'd quietly step out, hold the gun to the back of their heads, and pull the trigger. Exiting the alley on the waterfront, I'd throw the gun into the river and hightail it to Miss Charity's. I'd dreamed it so often it became second nature, and in my dreams, I felt no remorse.

Very weak, Miss Charity called me to her bedside and gave me joyous news that the wedding was scheduled for April eighteenth. She'd already made the arrangements for me to be in attendance.

We left camp just before noon on April sixteenth two days before the wedding. Elias, Matthew, Miss Charity, and I boarded a skiff headed down to the Apalachee Trail at the Jackson River Ford. A wagon and mules waited, and it was there I bid farewell to Elias with tears in my eyes. I watched as he rowed back toward his family.

***

It was mid-afternoon when we pulled up to Miss Charity's shack behind the Orman property. Mathew gently laid her in bed trying to make her as comfortable as possible. Miss Sadie was soon knocking on the door and was pleasantly surprised to find Matthew tending to his momma. The two of them embraced as though they were family of the same color. In the South, displays of affection for one's black family members would never be allowed out from behind closed doors.

Miss Sadie welcomed me and Miss Charity back as well but was anxious to tell the news of the Rebel Guard's kidnapping of Mr. Kohler and a Negro man named Stillman Smith. To date, their whereabouts was still unknown. I couldn't believe my ears and ran out of the shack down to Orman's dock. Leaping into a dingy, I headed up Scipio Creek. Matthew and Miss Sadie yelled at me to stop, but I knew an explanation would just waste precious time.

If my father and his cronies abducted Mr. Kohler, I figured they'd be holding him aboard the *Albany*. I rowed as fast as I could, slipping the dingy into the tall grass just shy of the *Albany*. I approached through the woods. All was quiet. There were footprints in the dirt and on the plank leading to the bow. Several men had been here not so long ago.

I moved from cabin to cabin, searching for Mr. Kohler. It was obvious men had slept here. I found my father's bedroll in his old cabin and gagged when I entered another. I knew this man just by his rancid smell—Aldridge. I was out of my mind with worry. I had to find Mr. Kohler. Filled with rage, I would leave this vermin no quarter. Soaking the bow with lantern oil, I set the *Albany* ablaze.

The wetlands of Scipio Creek were a sea of tall grass divided by a maze of channels. It was my good fortune to hear men's voices far off in the woods. I turned a bucket upside down on the seat of the dingy and stood on it so I might see over the grass toward the commotion. Six men, including Aldridge, were running toward the *Albany,* and now I knew where they were holed up; there was only one place between the *Albany* and town, and that was the slaughterhouse. I climbed down from the bucket and continued rowing back to town.

The *Albany* was made from the wood of the Long Leaf Pine, the same tree we turpentined. Locals called the wood by another name, "fat lighter;" light it with a match, and it would burn like a torch. I knew by the time they arrived, it would be burned to the waterline, and I would have scored another blow against the Rebel Guard.

The sun was set by the time I got back to the shack. I ran in, searching for my gun, but it was gone. Someone took my gun.

Matthew tried to convince me to stay with Miss Charity and let him join the search, but I told him I had to go. I knew where they were holding Mr. Kohler. Miss Charity called me to her bedside. I pleaded with her to return my gun. In a very weak voice, using all her strength, she told me her dying wish was that I never commit murder.

I ran from the shack down to Blood's Tavern and hid away in the alley. I had my jackknives opened, one in each hand, waiting for Dray or Aldridge to appear. My plan was foiled when Dray appeared in the street, choosing not to enter the alley. Instead, he stood out of my reach giving orders to two Rebel Guardsmen about how best to kill Mr. Kohler.

Blinded by fury, I ran out of the alley, screaming at the top of my lungs, "You leave Mr. Kohler alone!" I had every intention of sending him straight to perdition, driving my knives deep into his leg as I passed. Wrenching in pain, he turned and with the back of his hand knocked me unconscious.

***

It was Miss Dixie Belle who finally got a response out of me.

"What happened?" I puzzled.

"Dray done knocked you out girl," Dixie replied. "You been out for quite a while; I was gettin' worried."

My head was pounding as I sat up, but my only thought was my father had a head start. I had the dreadful feeling that all might be lost.

"I'd have taken you to Doc Chapman, but he's busy trying to take a bullet out that lady that runs the Florida Boarding House. You know her, that Miss Caroline."

"Is she alive?" I demanded to know.

"Calm yourself; they said she'd be fine, but that's more than I can say for that Aldridge fella. She blew his head clean off. It was a regular showdown right here on this very spot," Dixie explained.

My eyes were swollen and blurry when, out of the blue, Miss Dixie Belle said something most unexpected. "I'll be damned if that ain't Constable Jacob Foley walkin' this way."

She said it, and I couldn't hardly believe my ears. I called out in a loud voice. "Is that you, Jacob Foley?"

"Who hit you girl?" was his response. I recognized the voice of my angel.

I explained to him the circumstances and told him where they were holding our friend Mr. Kohler.

As I had written earlier, God is a force to be reckoned with. In Revelations, God called on the archangel Michael to go to war, and in the name of God, Michael defeated the devil himself. In my darkest hour, God sent me an archangel in the form of Jacob Foley. A glimmer of hope once again burned inside of me. Jacob immediately headed for the slaughter house.

I was soon on my feet, heading down to Doc Chapman's to check on Miss Caroline. Lottie and Ava were sitting on the porch and gave me a warm welcome while fussing over my blackened eyes. They told me Doctor Chapman assured them Miss Caroline would be alright. I told them I was seeing to Mr. Kohler's release and was confident she and Mr. Kohler would soon be reunited.

Turning, I left, heading for the slaughterhouse. By the time I arrived, Mr. Kohler was free, and he and Jacob were standing in judgment over Dray at the end of the dock. I knew this had to be done.

Riddled with guilt, I vomited and lamented over what was about to happen. I watched as Mr. Kohler raised the gun to the back of Dray's head. There were four separate flashes, each followed a second later by a loud report.

It was finally over, but God chose to send me one more sign, and I watched as Hickory rose from the water catching Dray in midair, dragging him to Hell. As it was written in Revelations 6:8, it was "with the beasts of the earth" that Dray met his end. At least that's the way it appeared to a girl of nine.

The sun was rising, and I remained hidden in the woods, watching as Captain Hatch approached with the townspeople close behind. I found my second wind when I saw Miss Caroline arrive by wagon. Townspeople helped her down so that she might embrace Mr. Kohler as he approached from the dock. I was beaten and bruised with two black eyes, but I'd never felt better than when I ran up and, once again, looked into Miss Caroline's beautiful face. I truly felt as though it was a family reunion.

After a visit to Doctor Chapman, I asked him to come down to check on Miss Charity, telling him that if he could save her, I would give him all the gold I had. As it turned out, there are some things gold just can't buy. Looking back, I realized he had no idea what I was offering. In the end, it made no difference. Gold or not, he did the best he could. Miss Charity passed away at three o'clock on the day of the wedding. I was with her as she breathed her last.

Wandering down to the church, I sat on a bench out of sight, not wanting to dampen the festivities with my sadness. Miss Lottie found me and insisted on calling Miss Caroline. Soon, Mr. Kohler joined us and became ill, vomiting, when I confessed to Dray being my real father.

Riddled with guilt over the role he played in Dray's death, he never brought himself to confess his deed. Mr. Kohler and Miss Caroline adopted me, and we became the family I imagined. It was the first time in my life I had a real father and mother. It was a relief to have people I loved, to share in the golden bounty I had found. My new father taught me as his father taught him, eventually sending me off to Wesleyan Ladies College for a more formal education.

The great fortune I had found remained in my keep, and father taught me the responsibility that goes along with great wealth. If today I'm considered a good steward, the credit would fall to my father.

I married for love, a good and decent man, in June of 1872. My daughter, Olivia, was born in April of the following year. Olivia grew up supported by a loving family.

Tragedy struck in 1880 when my husband died of consumption. It was through the love and power of strong family that we survived those hard times. Eventually, even this tragedy served to strengthen our family bonds.

After the War of Rebellion, and the bullet passed through Mr. Lincoln's head, the drunkard Andrew Johnson came to power, and the cause of freedom I fought for was set back by decades with the new President's black codes and laws. "This is a country for white men, and by God, as long as I am President, it shall be a government for white men," he wrote in 1866.

Northern businessmen bought up Southern industries and land from a totally devastated South. Between the remaining Southern aristocracy and those men from the North, it wasn't long before they realized they would never survive without slavery. Slavery was reintroduced into the South in the form of peonage and convict leasing.

Slaves, once thought of as hard working and loyal, were now free and labeled as a people of sloth and deceit. They were arrested by corrupt law enforcement for trumped-up charges such as vagrancy, fined unreasonable amounts which could never be paid, and sold out of jails by local judges to the lumber camp, turpentine camp, and coal mine, with the highest bid. With no chance of paying the fines, they would never be released from the camps to which they had been sold.

The old battle against slavery paled in comparison to the new battle against this more organized and sophisticated form of slavery. My daughter, Oliva, is choosing to become a warrior in this new battle; at times, I am so proud I cry. I only hope that through this new battle, I may in some way seek forgiveness for my sinful life and pave a path to heaven.

Chapter XIX

"Truth Will Make You Free"

Make no mistake; we were Confederates in the true sense of the word. We supported the Confederate States of America's right to secede from the Union.

Most citizens of the South did not own slaves, and supporting slavery had little to do with being a loyal Confederate. We simply didn't like being told what to do and how to live our lives by a bunch of arrogant Yankees. We were tired of being pillaged, having to watch as Southern dollars moved north to support an industrial economy.

It was unfortunate that the smaller, slave-holding aristocracy of the south also controlled our new government and used it for their own greedy, short-term interests—a pattern that I find has been repeated throughout history.

The father at my conception was Guillaume Gauthier Verheist, better known as Dray. I consider my adoptive father, Michael Brandon Kohler to be my true father. He was the one who cared for and nurtured me growing up.

Much to my objections, Michael Brandon Kohler, recently passed from this world. I have read his journal and now find myself weeping for this poor unfortunate man who, by virtue of his kindness, was burdened with the task of loving me.

Nothing is as it seems. I will not allow my father to bear an undeserved burden of guilt. What my father wrote in his journal was not a lie, but on occasion, the records of history need to be amended by someone who stood a few feet away with a slightly different view of events. As my father chronicled, "We sit like gods on the pinnacle of our lies, convinced of our own omnipotence, and then too late realize it is through truth we will find enlightenment. Many will seek the grace that is God, but few will find it. I grow tired of my own lies and now wish to be one of the few."

"And ye shall know the truth, and the truth shall make you free." John 8:32.

I once saw a man shoot his finest hound, and with a tear in his eye, he told me that good or bad, we are responsible for the creatures in our charge. His dear friend and companion was in great pain, and he took it upon himself to end the suffering.

It is the blood of Guillaume Gauthier Verheist that flows in my veins; he was a cruel, murderous man without conscience. When I mournfully realized he was incapable of love, it was I who chose the time and method of his execution. It was I who stood in the shadows lamenting as Mr. Kohler pulled that trigger. It is I who am responsible for Dray's death. At what age does God hold a child accountable?

History is never as it seems. As my father once wrote, "I now see that the history we write is like the river that flows through my town; it has great power but always seeks the easy path."

As my father before me, it is through these words, I amend the unseen truths of my life. I am Pearl, it is July 10th, 1903.

As my father recorded in his journal, "History written by men reveals no cowards except those of the enemy, tells of great deeds of worth and cause, but shows only one face and fails to distinguish the testimony of those consumed by its passing."

It is a thought that appeared many times throughout history.

"History is a set of lies agreed upon."
Napoleon Bonaparte

"I'm not upset that you lied to me; I'm upset that from now on, I can't believe you."
Friedrich Nietzsche

"Anything is better than lies and deceit!"
Leo Tolstoy, Anna Karenina

"In thy foul throat thou liest."
William Shakespeare, Richard III

"A lie that is half-truth is the darkest of all lies."
Alfred Tennyson

"No man has a good enough memory to be a successful liar."
Abraham Lincoln

"Those who are capable of tyranny are capable of perjury to sustain it."
Lysander Spooner

"You can fool some of the people all of the time, and all of the people some of the time, but you cannot fool all of the people all of the time."
Abraham Lincoln

To acquire possessions, to maintain wealth, protection of pride, malice, self-preservation, embellishment, are these truly justifications for lying? At some point, all people lie, even children. We are born into the world with no barter except the sound of a crying voice, it is a cry that triggers a parent's primal instinct to nurture. It is an ancient instinct endowed to parents by God to protect children.

Babies and children quickly learn to use crying as a tool, lying, manipulating their parents to get what they want. Conscience is instilled in children by parents, with the hope it will separate the lies from truth, guiding them in later life.

I have been nearly two years writing this account. I often found myself reliving events too painful to bear—walking away for months at a time, believing I may never complete the task.

The facts will soon bear out that I have lied even in these accounts. In honor of my father, Michael Brandon Kohler, I will try and reveal the truth of events known to no one but me. The truth can be a bitter brew to swallow.

***

At the wharves in Apalachicola, in the eighteen thirties and early forties, if you called out for a Dray—one of the many wagons that shifted the freight—on my father's wagon, two men would come to your beck and call. For the most part, they were interchangeable and inseparable, my father, Guillaume, and his brother, Alexandre. At work, they both answered to the same name, Dray.

The day I burned the *Albany,* I was surprised to see Alexandre leading the pack down the shoreline, heading for the burning steamer. I knew it was him, having seen him once before when we visited my Aunt Etta.

The brothers worked together to pillage St. Joseph after it fell to the Yellow Fever epidemic of 1841, but for reasons unknown, they had a falling out and separated for years, unwilling to reconcile. I can only speculate that Etta and greed had something to do with their reunion. It would have been like Etta to play them against one another for her own gain.

Other than Miss Dixie Belle, I imagined there were few people who remembered my father had a brother, and even Dixie was confused, believing it was my father who had been bested by Mr. Kohler that night at Blood's Tavern. It was in fact, Alexandre who took the beating. Separated by one year and having the same mother and father, they carried a remarkable resemblance to one another.

Looking back, I cannot remember a time when I did not lie, sometimes even to myself. Lies are a place one can hide unbearable pain.

It is only in my dreams that on the night of my altercation with Aldridge, Elias showed up in time, but he didn't. That disgusting, stinking creature had his way with me. Elias pulled him off just after he finished satisfying himself at my expense.

I could have expected little else. I grew up in places not fit for a child with a father who was cold and uncaring. I wish I could record that Aldridge was the only time I had been raped, but that would be a lie.

Knowing of my circumstances, if people knew the truth, they would have looked upon me as being impure and a whore. The last thing on the mind of an eight year old should have been living down the stigma of being a whore, but these were the cards I was dealt, so I lied.

I wish I could tell you that in all my rage I was unsuccessful in my murderous attempts and never took a life, but that would be a lie. There were five of the Rebel Guard on the *Albany,* sleeping off a drunken stupor.

I started with the lower cabins on the first deck so the blood would not rain down through the floorboard into the cabins below. One by one, with a razor-sharp knife, I slit their throats.

Slitting a throat is not what I expected. I knew from seeing my father's victims that the cut had to be deep enough to slice one or both of the arteries in the neck, and the knife blade needed to be long enough so when drawn across the throat, it would also sever the wind pipe.

Cutting though the wind pipe insured there would be no alarm. The only noise was the sound of air whistling from the lungs. A couple of them were so drunk, they didn't have much of a reaction. To be quite honest, I fully expected to be caught and killed, and that was fine with me.

It was to my good fortune that the *Albany* was large, and the cabins were separated by other cabins or compartments. It served well to muffle the sounds of struggle put up by the next two men. Surprisingly, I knew they saw me, but they were so busy holding their throats, trying to keep the blood in, they never once threatened to harm me but rather stared with a look of puzzlement.

In the cabin above on the third deck slept my father. He didn't even stir as I opened the door, held the Pepperbox to the back of his head, and spilled his brains. He immediately rolled over on his back, but after that, he didn't seem to be able to move at all. He gazed at me in disbelief.

I stood for a moment staring at him, but all I could see was Bella laying on that table with her throat slit and the image I had created in my mind of Basher bloated with his nose, ears, and eyes, eaten away by the crabs and gulls. I thought of Mr. Freud and his wife Ida, murdered after having been so kind to me. The most disturbing image that I could only imagine was of Odila and Zelig locked forever in amber with a look of terror frozen in their eyes.

Leaning over him, I softly spoke, "You killed my friends." I then tried to make him proud by demonstrating one of the lessons he had taught me; just for good measure, I slit his throat.

I burned the *Albany* to cover my tracks, and let me assure you, the fire was hot enough to burn bone.

Having seen the men running down the shoreline, I knew they had to be holding Mr. Kohler at the slaughterhouse. I also knew he was my last best chance at leading a better life.

Alexandre was there for Etta to keep an eye on my father and share in the bounty the family placed on my head. I knew I would find no peace as long as he was alive.

When I arrived back at the shack, Miss Charity and Matthew had hidden my powder, shot, and tools, so I was unable to reload. After my failed attempt to dispose of Alexandre down at Blood's Tavern, it was just by the grace of God that Jacob showed up in my darkest hour.

Many would have you believe that the Bible says, "Thou shalt not kill," but in the original Hebrew, it was written, "Thou shalt not murder," and did not apply to war or penalties of death for unspeakable crimes against humanity. God himself ordered many wars and a penalty of death for numerous crimes. This was my war, and it was the only way to keep evil men from harming the innocent.

My life changed dramatically after the events at the slaughterhouse. I hid the truth deep inside, far away from the light of day. Never again would I raise my hand in anger as I did that day on the *Albany* so many years ago.

At what age does God hold a child accountable? History is never as it seems.

When I die, I will leave mine and my father's journals in the hands of my daughter, Olivia. I'll not allow her to live believing in the lies I endured for so many years.

I will also leave her a map that will lead her to the chamber that to this day still contains the lion's share of the gold. I may have also misled the reader in the actual location of the chamber. The justification for this lie is simple. It's none of your concern. She is a responsible young woman who will make us all proud, and I am confident she will make a fine steward.

The End

Postscript:

In my writings, I have omitted the mention of the Negro, Stillman Smith. Stillman played an important role in my father's life, but I regret to say I scarcely knew him. One thing I have learned over the years is that bloodline has very little to do with family. The darkest hours of the Terrible War played an important role in the union of my father Michael Kohler with his true brother, the freed Negro, Stillman Smith. Their family bond, forged in the fires of war, transcended death. At the end of Father's life, with decrepitude reaping a toll on his body and mind, he would awaken at night screaming Stillman's name. Then sitting in the darkness, he would once again mourn the loss of his brother.

I regret that I did not know Stillman Smith as well as my father. I knew he worked with my father as a free man and of his own accord, but little did I know, we were allies in the same battle against slavery. Stillman's gift to me was one of time. While Dray and his Rebel Guard debated over the method of Stillman's death, rescue was able to reach my father. I leave the story of Stillman to my father's accounting of events but will never discount the important role Stillman Smith played in my family's history.

Pearl

References

Willoughby, Lynn. Fair to Middlin': The Antebellum Cotton Trade of the Apalachicola / Chattahoochee River Valley. University of Alabama Press, Tuscaloosa, Alabama. 1993.

Sherlock, Vivian. The Fever Man: A Biography of Dr. John Gorrie. V. M. Sherlock. 1982.

Zinn, Howard. A People's History of the United States: 1492 to Present. Harper Perennial Modern Classics. New York. 2005.

Nichols, Jimmie J. "1836 —1986 Sesquicentennial History of Trinity Episcopal Church, Apalachicola, Florida," Jimmie J. Nichols. 1987.

Smith, Julia Floyd. Slavery and Plantation Growth in Antebellum Florida 1821 —1860. University Press of Florida. Gainesville, Florida. 1973.

Rogers, William Warren. Outposts on the Gulf: Saint George Island & Apalachicola from Early Exploration to World War II. University of West Florida Press. Pensacola, Florida. 1986

Mueller, Edward A. Perilous Journeys: A History of Steamboating on the Chattahoochee, Apalachicola, and Flint Rivers, 1828 — 1928. Historic Chattahoochee. 1990.

Turner, Maxine. Naval Operations on the Apalachicola and Chattahoochee Rivers 1861 — 1865. Alabama Historical Quarterly. 1975.

Rose, P.K. The Civil War: Black American Contributions to Union intelligence. CIA Center for the Study of Intelligence. U.S. Government. Washington. D.C. 2007.

Orman family, for archive materials.

Owens, Harry P. "Apalachicola Before 1861." Florida State University, PhD. Dissertation. University Microfilms, Inc., Ann Arbor, Michigan. 1966. (Thank You Harry)

John Milton to Col. W. J. Magill, Feb. 20, 1864. Milton Letterbook, 44, Florida State Archives, Tallahassee. OR Union and Confederate Navies in the War of the Rebellion, Series I, Vol. 17, 350.

The city of Apalachicola, Florida, and the wonderful people who cherish and preserve its history.

Douglas A. Blackmon Slavery by another Name: (The re-enslavement of black Americas from the Civil War to World War II. Publisher Anchor.

Photo Credits

Library of Congress, Prints and Photographs Division, Page Washington, D.C. 20540 USA.
The U.S.M. Mississippi passenger steamer,
By, Charles Graham.

Credit for the following photos to the State Archives of Florida "Florida Memory Project:

RC11531 Confederate Crossing
Artist's rendering of Confederate cavalrymen crossing the St. John's River. 1865. Black & white photoprint, 8 x 10 in. State Archives of Florida, Florida Memory.
<https://www.floridamemory.com/items/show/34038>, accessed 12 February 2017.

RC03347 Destruction of the Salt Works\
Destruction of a rebel salt factory, on the Florida coast. 1862. Black & white photoprint, 8 x 10 in. State Archives of Florida, Florida Memory.
<https://www.floridamemory.com/items/show/26985>, accessed 12 February 2017.

PR08511 Ira Sanborn
Portrait of Ira Sanborn. 18--. Black & white photograph, 4 x 6 in. State Archives of Florida, Florida Memory.
<https://www.floridamemory.com/items/show/7048>, accessed 12 February 2017.

N046490 Trinity Church
Trinity Episcopal Church - Apalachicola, Florida. 1884. Black & white photonegative, 4 x 5 in. State Archives of Florida, Florida Memory.
<https://www.floridamemory.com/items/show/154416>, accessed 12 February 2017.

N040482 River Bride
Steamboat, City of Jacksonville on the Saint Johns River. 19--. Black & white photonegative, 4 x 5 in. State Archives of Florida, Florida Memory. <https://www.floridamemory.com/items/show/148699>, accessed 12 February 2017.

Orman Family Archive. Slave Quarters,

Allen & Thurber Pepperbox, Wikipedia. Page

About the Author

After a working career and raising two daughters, my wife and I moved to the Florida Panhandle. It was in the historic town of Apalachicola that I began creating and caring for the Orman House State Park Museum. When I started, the house was an empty shell. Immersed in local history, I now enjoy sharing Apalachicola's rich heritage with thousands of visitors from around the world. Apalachicola Pearl and Apalachicola Gold were born from my passion for the town's history and its people. My sincere wish is for you to enjoy reading the books as much as I enjoyed writing them.